THE LATECOMER

To Ariel

Also by Sarah Aldridge:
TOTTIE
CYTHEREA'S BREATH
ALL TRUE LOVERS
THE NESTING PLACE

SARAH ALDRIDGE   Photo by Tee A. Corinne

THE LATECOMER

by Sarah Aldridge

THE NAIAD PRESS

1982

THE LATECOMER
By
SARAH ALDRIDGE

PART I

The day was quiet and grey. Just the sort of day, Philippa thought, that you would expect on the English Channel late in October. The Southampton quayside was wide, stony, deserted, and Philippa felt the gentle melancholy of the place and occasion settle on her like a mantle. She knew it was a melancholy woven of a number of strands—her awareness of the end of her holiday, the (at the moment) uninviting prospect of once more teaching philology to college students, the demands and restrictions of a working life. There was one more, always there latent but sometimes, as now, surfacing unbidden, the knowledge that there was no one who had any intimate interest in her absence or her return. She contemplated this last steadily for a little while, as she always did when it came to the fore-front of her mind, then dismissed it once more. It was simply her nature to be solitary. She had experienced such moments of depression often enough in the last twenty years and she knew that they passed quickly with the upsurge of energy that came with her taking up the regular duties of her life after a holiday.

She waited in the passenger lounge of the pier until the officials were ready to check the papers of those boarding the huge ship whose side towered over the quayside. By then there was a crowd of people and the quiet of the great spaces was filled with the clamor of voices and the sounds of mechanical devices. By nature unaggressive and still caught up in her feeling of withdrawal from her surroundings, Philippa made no effort to place herself in the front of the throng queueing at the purser's desk. She was traveling first class, an extravagance she would find it hard to explain to the Dimocks who were in tourist. True, it was only the bottom of firstclass, the most that she could afford but Trudy would not fail to resent it.

As she stepped up in her turn to the purser's desk she remembered the question about her stateroom. It was not a single cabin. There had been none left, when she applied for passage months ago, in the range of price she could afford. But when she had made her reservation she had been assured that probably, since this was a westward sailing well after the end of the season, she would have it to herself.

The purser's assistant, examining her ticket, said, "One moment" and turned away for a private consultation with a colleague. When he returned to her he said, "You will have another lady with you in the stateroom." It was someone, he explained, who had booked passage at the last moment and wanted just this sort of accommodation.

Philippa, disappointed, thought, she must be someone like me, without enough money for a better stateroom but wanting first class nevertheless. The purser's assistant was saying something defensive, but she waved it aside. I could not expect them to turn down another passenger for my convenience. She was passed quickly on to the diningroom steward, who said she had been placed at a large table with five others. If she wished to make a change she could make a request after the ship sailed.

She went at once to find the stateroom and arrange her belongings. It was on Three Deck, a narrow room with two beds placed with their heads to the wall, with a small table between them. A dressing table just within the door, a wardrobe opposite and the bathroom at the inner end of the room completed the scene. There was no sign of her cabinmate. Which bed should she appropriate for herself? The one under the portholes? Or should she really wait for her companion to arrive and consult with her? If she only knew what sort of person her roommate was—someone eager and ready to grasp the advantage, or someone retiring, likely to be overridden by a more forceful personality. If she settled things now, singlehanded, would she then have to contend throughout the voyage with someone who was resentful and vocal about it or someone who would silently reproach her? Either way it would be a nuisance. Her bid for luxury in ship travel would be subtly spoiled.

Why, Philippa asked herself, do I have to be burdened with this self-examining temperament, especially now? I'm almost forty. Why can't I simply do what I want to do and forget about somebody else's reactions?

She ended by taking her clothes from her suitcase and hanging them carefully in one half of the wardrobe. Her other articles she placed neatly in the bottom drawer of the dressing-table. Her toilet articles she disposed in one of the two small drawers at the top. She habitually traveled light and after a summer spent in the more primitive regions of eastern Europe she had little luggage. One dinner dress to meet the requirements of first class on a Cunarder, a heavy woolen suit to meet the cold of late autumn on arrival in New York, the slacks and sweaters she had worn in the mountains—that was really all she had. Having disposed of her clothes, she stood gazing once more at the beds. She would prefer the bed under the portholes. A seasoned ship traveler, she was never seasick. Nor did she as a rule require the bathroom during the night. So that, if she took the further bed, it was unlikely that she would need to disturb her companion by stepping past the other bed.

But these arguments, spoken to herself, lacked the power to sway her to the point of action. She gave the problem up and decided to go on deck and watch the activities of late-arriving passengers. For the next hour or so she was entertained by the cheerful bustle of embarkation. Now and again her mind reverted to the unknown woman with whom she was to share her more intimate moments for the next five days. The two beds presented themselves to her inner eye. The trouble was, she thought, that she had never had this problem before. Whenever she had traveled before she had either been alone or with friends, discreet, reticent friends, as shy of physical contact as she herself. Otherwise she had never lived intimately with anyone except her mother and father, staid, reserved people. She had not been to boarding school and when it was time to go to college, she had lived at home and attended classes as a day student.

Though the problem nagged at her, she was reluctant to go down to the stateroom and possibly confront that stranger, arriving bag and baggage. But finally the moment came when all but the last lines attaching the ship to the wharf were cast off and the loudspeakers were urging visitors to go ashore. She turned away from the rail and watched a large, noisy party of people, no longer aware of the place or purpose of their conviviality, whom various stewards and ship's officers were politely but firmly pressing towards the last gangway. She could not determine who it was who was being seen off, except that this was apparently a woman. With sudden decision Philippa left the deck and found her way down stairways and along corridors until she reached the stateroom.

At the door she stopped and listened. No sound came through the panel, except the muted voice on the intercom repeating the last call for going ashore. Philippa suppressed her instinct to knock—she told herself that it was absurd to knock for admittance to her own stateroom—and opened the door.

At first she had a fleeting thought that she had mistaken the room. The air was saturated with scent—French perfume mingled with that of a couple of large bouquets, one of long-stemmed roses and the other of gardenias, combined with the smell of whiskey and stale cigarette smoke. Of all the hazards that had occurred to her, this had not. She stood in the middle of the small floorspace and surveyed the transformation of the primly neat room she had last seen. The ashtrays on the dressing-table and the bedside stand all held cigarette butts and ash and the glasses that had been neatly arranged on the tray with the water decanter had been used and left about wherever the user had stood or sat. Two large airplane suitcases stood in front of the wardrobe. The bed under the porthole was laden with a woman's light coat, an air travel bag, two or three paperback books, a travel umbrella with a shiny chrome metal chain. The coverlet on the other bed was rumpled as if several people had sat there. An expensive white leather dressing case lay there also. The gold letters on it shone up at her: Katherine Armitage Stephens.

So absorbed was she in assessing what all this meant that she jumped at the bellow of the ship's departing signal. She was too far down in the vessel to hear the voices of the shore-going visitors. But the rumble of the last gangway being withdrawn told her that the great ship was ready to move out into the waterway. While she stood there uncertainly someone spoke at her back. She had forgotten that she had left the door open.

"Is this where I belong? Oh, yes, it must be."

The young woman who spoke was standing wide-eyed in the doorway, gazing at her and at the room with bright blue eyes that reflected the sea beyond the portholes. She is not yet thirty, thought Philippa, or not more than a year or two beyond. And how pretty!

The newcomer said, "I'm Kay Stephens. Phoo! What an awful fug!"

She sprang across the narrow space past Philippa and seized the big screw that closed the porthole.

Philippa said, "I think it is locked shut. You will have to get the steward to open it—if he will."

"Why won't he?"

"Ring for him and see," said Philippa, pointing to the button for the bell.

While they waited Kay said, "I never can understand why some women can't restrain themselves where it comes to perfume. It should be subtle. But Norene douses herself with anything she gets in Paris and when you mix it with a couple of others in a small space—Good God! Whoever sent gardenias? Maybe I can get the steward to take them away." She paused as if at a sudden thought. "You don't want them, do you?"

"The roses will do very well for me. The room is rather small. My name, by the way, is Philippa Weir."

Kay, her ear picking up the accent and precision of Philippa's voice, gave her a moment's stare before she said, "Well, hello, Philippa." Then she took a comb out of her handbag and stood in front of the looking-glass combing the long pale blonde hair that hung almost to her shoulders.

Neither of them spoke until a stewardess tapped softly on the open door. Then Philippa said, "Would it be possible to open the portholes, or one of them? And can you take these away? They are rather overpowering."

The stewardess went away with the gardenias, glancing first at the used tumblers and the full ashtrays, saying that she would tell the steward, who might have a key to the porthole screw. Philippa looked again at the bed under the portholes and debated briefly whether to mention it. But she did not and sat down on the other bed, gently pushing aside the dressing case.

"You understand," she said, "that means a special tip."

Kay paused in what she was doing. "You're used to ship travel, aren't you?"

"I've been on a number of sea trips."

"I've never been on a ship before. I've always gone by air."

"Then you may get impatient."

"Impatient?" Kay's voice held surprise, as if this idea had never crossed her mind.

"But perhaps you have friends on board."

"No." Kay turned away from the looking-glass to gaze at her. "That crowd you saw just came to see me off."

"That crowd?" Philippa glanced around at the disordered room. "No, I did not see them."

They were interrupted by the steward. He was a short, smiling man with a cockney accent, who opened the portholes while admonishing them of the dire consequences of leaving the glass open if the weather should worsen. Philippa watched as he and Kay fell into lively conversation, his quick eyes taking in her appearance, his volubility increasing in response to something in her that roused his interest as a man. I wonder, thought Philippa, why she has chosen to come by ship.

The question prompted her to look again at Kay's luggage. It was expensive and fashionable. And the dresses and pantsuits and shoes that Kay now began to pull out of the cases had been bought in the sort of shops that wealthy women patronized. But there were not a great many of them. In fact, Kay seemed not to have many more clothes than she did herself. Of course, perhaps this simply came from the habit of traveling by air. Nevertheless, Philippa had a vague sense that this was not a woman of means. Perhaps she is an actress, she thought, or someone who must maintain an appearance of affluence. That would account for her traveling first class, even at the bottom of the fare scale.

The steward had left and the stewardess came back with a fresh tray and glasses and emptied the ashtrays. By now Kay was in the bathroom and the stateroom had reverted to something of the quiet orderliness that Philippa had first seen.

But not quite. The fresh breeze from the open portholes had swept away the heavy mixture of gardenias and French perfume and stale smoke. The fresh scent of the roses lingered and there was a subtle aroma of someone else's presence. Kay's belongings still lay on the bed under the porthole and the dressing case still occupied the center of the other bed.

Philippa sat for another few moments gazing about. Then, obeying a sudden impulse, she got up and left the stateroom. She sought the promenade deck and a view of the Solent and the Isle of Wight, an impersonal landscape. The clouds that had so smoothly covered the sky during the morning were now broken and a filtered sunlight gleamed on the water. There were vessels all around them, of every size and age. As she watched the crowded waterway widened and grew emptier. For a long time she stood by the rail, unwilling to go back down stairs in spite of the chill wind that gradually seeped through her warm woolen suit. At last, too chilled to stay longer, she found the nearest stairway and ducked inside. She found herself on an enclosed deck where people were sitting about at small tables busy with tea or drinks. She hesitated for a moment, debating whether to prolong her stay away from the stateroom but the babble of voices discouraged her. She was turning away to go through the doorway to another staircase when someone suddenly put a hand on her arm and said, "Philippa!"

She looked at the woman who had stopped her. "Hello, Trudy." She hoped Trudy did not notice her lack of warmth. But Trudy rarely noticed such things. "Guess what, Phil? Until this evening, after we have left Cherbourg, we serfs from tourist class have the run of the ship! After this evening you will have to come below stairs to see us. I still don't understand why you insisted on crossing first class. You've never acted like a snob before. Besides, life isn't nearly so stuffy in tourist."

Philippa, irritated, said, "I'm not being a snob. Trudy, I've already explained to you. I made my reservations last winter, before I knew that you and Lawrence would be coming back at the same time."

"Well, we had the whole summer together. That was fun." Trudy was still looking at her avidly, as if to satisfy her curiosity by sight if not by words. She was a small woman, with reddish hair and a snub nose. But her most striking features were her greenish-blue eyes that constantly darted here and there, taking in every detail of the people and scene around her. She is convinced, thought Philippa, that I have deliberately chosen to travel first class to escape her and Lawrence. And she is right, of course. I wanted this time to myself before getting back to Deerfield. And I want a taste of luxury. Trudy would love to trap me into admitting this.

"Oh, well, " said Trudy, good naturedly, "Why don't you join us for a drink now."

"Not now, Trudy, thank you." Philippa's reluctance to return to the stateroom had vanished in her greater anxiety to escape Trudy.

When she got there it was to find the stateroom empty, except for the subtle signs of Kay's presence—the scent of the roses mingling with that of the soap Kay had used, the belongings still strewn on the beds. With a feeling of vexation that surprised herself, she lifted the dressing case from the near bed and placed it on the bed under the portholes, with the other objects. Then, aware that the long wait to board ship, the standing about watching the preparations for departure, the chilling she had endured on the open deck had made her tired and dispirited, she lay down on the bed and drew the coverlet over her. She doubted if she would sleep but the peace and quiet tempted her.

When she opened her eyes and remembered where she was she knew that she had been asleep for some time. The stateroom was still quiet. If Kay—she had fallen easily into thinking of her roommate as simply Kay—had come back, she had been very quiet about it. Philippa was aware that there was something different about the ship's movement. The engines had slowed. They must have reached the French coast and presumably were entering Cherbourg harbor. A glance out of the porthole told her her surmise was correct.

It was too chilly on the open deck for most people. Philippa, walking about to keep warm, reached the side out of the wind. Another woman was standing there at the rail alone, watching the little activity there was to be seen. When the woman turned her head she saw it was Kay.

"Well, hi!" said Kay. "Do you know how long we'll be here?"

"A couple of hours or so."

"We're going to have a gale, one of the officers told me. It's coming out of the Irish Sea. I hope I'm not seasick."

"You've been very lucky with the Channel crossing. It is seldom so calm. Do you have some dramamine or something of that sort?"

Kay gave a nervous little laugh. "Do you think I should take it now?"

"I don't know. Have you ever been seasick?"

"No. But then I've never been on the ocean."

"Then why don't we wait?"

Kay, hearing the "we", thought, what a charming smile. She certainly isn't what I thought she would be. When they told me that I had a roommate and that she was a college professor, I thought she'd be sixty and grey-haired and crotchety. But she isn't. She's a little starchy, but maybe—That suit she is wearing shows a real sense of style.

"Well, I hope you won't regret that advice," Kay said aloud.

"Let's not think about it. Seasickness is said to be at least partly psychological."

They were silent for a while, watching the gulls circling over the placid, grey-green water of the harbor. The afternoon had settled into a quiet greyness, with only an occasional gleam of pale sunlight. The quay alongside which the great ship slowly moved was almost deserted. Beyond it lay the town, the houses and streets climbing the gentle hills.

Kay said then, "Would you like to come and have a drink?"

"Why, yes. Perhaps it would make things a little more cheerful. It is a dreary afternoon, isn't it?"

"Oh, you think so, too? I thought maybe it was just me."

They found their way into one of the bars. It was crowded and filled with the sound of many voices. But eventually they got a table in a corner that was quiet enough to permit conversation. They both ordered scotch, but Kay said a double on the rocks and Philippa specified water.

As they waited, Kay looked at Philippa. A beam of late sunlight reached into their corner and lit up her face. She has a beautiful skin, thought Kay, and lovely eyes, a grey-blue, with those long lashes. She doesn't use cosmetics, so it must all be real.

Philippa, uneasy under her scrutiny, said, "Are you crossing by sea just out of curiosity?"

"Well, yes, I suppose so. But then, I'm at a loose end. It was a whim, really. The people I've been with couldn't understand why I wanted to come this way. It's so boring, they said. I didn't tell them I had a roommate. That would really have knocked them."

Philippa looked at her uncertainly but said nothing.

Kay found herself talking on, nervously. "As a matter of fact, when they told me you were a college professor, I thought I was in for five days with somebody who'd fuss about liquor and cigarettes and draughts."

Philippa's voice was sharp. "Perhaps I shan't disappoint you."

Wow! thought Kay. She can bite! Aloud she said, "Well, obviously you don't mind liquor." She smiled to try to dissipate the coldness in Philippa's face.

For a moment Philippa resisted the unspoken apology. Then she relaxed and took a sip of her drink. "Is this also the first time you have been in Europe?"

"Yes. I've been in Rome and London for a couple of months. We've been shooting scenes for the second sequence." Seeing the question in Philippa's face, she went on, "I'm a film editor. I thought perhaps you had recognized my name."

Philippa thought, perhaps I should have. Or perhaps it is only youthful vanity. Aloud she said, "I'm sorry. I'm not a very frequent movie goer. It must be interesting—film editing."

Kay looked at her from under her eyebrows, a little sulky. "It's food and drink and everything else to me. What have you been doing in Europe—touring the museums?"

Philippa's glance was faintly satirical. "I've done that many times before. No. I was in eastern Europe, looking for traces of Latin and other ancient languages in the speech of the modern inhabitants of those regions."

Kay opened her eyes wide and laughed. "I have trouble enough with modern French and Italian."

"Well, tell me. What does a film editor do?"

Kay looked at her suspiciously but there was nothing in Philippa's face except polite curiosity. "You realize," she began and then broke off. "Perhaps you don't know. When a film is made, there are often many different versions shot of a scene. When the film is all done it is my job to go through it with all the reshots and put together the best, the ones I think project best what the director had in mind. I was just an observer at this stage—watching the film being shot. I'll do my job later, when the film is all ready."

"It sounds rather complicated," Philippa murmured. "It would be like—weaving a tapestry."

Kay looked at her in surprise. "Why, I suppose you could say so. Of course, in mediaeval times tapestries were often scenarios, weren't they?"

Philippa suddenly smiled. "That's very clever of you."

Kay blushed and was silent for a few moments. Finally she said, "By the way, I'm sorry you found the stateroom such a shambles. But I didn't tell anybody it wasn't all mine. They knew I wouldn't care what a mess they made. None of them think they can celebrate anything without getting stoned."

"That's all right. I was a little surprised. But I understand now."

There was another pause and then Philippa said, "I think we have been placed at the same table for dinner tonight. But tomorrow you can ask for another assignment."

"I don't know anybody on board—yet. Are you going to change?"

"I see no reason to. I have friends aboard but they are in tourist."

Again they lapsed into silence. Philippa thought, she seems to expect to make friends right away. Kay thought, if I meet somebody, it is a cinch I won't be able to finish the night in the stateroom. It will have to be his.

After a while Kay said, "There seems to be someone over there who is trying to attract your attention."

Philippa glanced where she pointed and saw Trudy gesticulating from a table where she sat with Lawrence and a tall old man. Philippa waved back, hoping earnestly that Trudy would be satisfied with this recognition and stay where she was. But that, after all, would be quite unlike Trudy.

In a few minutes Trudy had found her way through the thronged room to stand by their table. "Why, Phil, we were hoping you'd come and join us." As she spoke her quick, darting eyes moved to Kay and back to Philippa.

"I'm sorry, Trudy. I did not expect to come here for a drink. Trudy, this is my roommate, Kay Stephens."

Trudy said brightly, "How do you do?" and this time her eyes stayed fixed on Kay. "I think I saw you come aboard."

Philippa recognized the remark as one charged with some withheld comment. I'll hear what that is the next time I'm alone with Trudy, she thought. Trudy stood beside their table for a few more minutes, exchanging commonplaces, before she returned to her own table.

As she left, Kay said, "One of your friends?"

"Yes. I spent the summer with Trudy and her husband."

"Philologizing?"

"I was philologizing. They—they have other disciplines."

Kay smiled sweetly. "It's too complicated to explain it all to me, isn't it?"

Philippa, embarrassed, said hastily, "I don't suppose it would interest you very much."

Kay still smiled. "You are not a great talker, are you?" She was suddenly serious. "But talking isn't the only way to communicate, is it? In fact, sometimes it is the least useful."

"That is quite a profound statement."

This time Kay laughed.

They did not return to the stateroom together. By the time the first call for dinner sounded Philippa was dressed and ready to go to the diningroom. There was still no sign of Kay. She wondered, as she fastened the bracelet on her wrist, whether Kay had stayed in the bar. In retrospect she had come to the conclusion that Kay had had her share of the liquor that had flowed so freely amongst those who had come to see her off.

The motion of the ship had become more marked. We must be reaching the mouth of the Irish Sea, thought Philippa. The gale is coming out of there. On her way to the diningroom she paused in the main lounge to read the ship's notices about the weather. There would be gale force northwest winds when they passed the tip of Ireland into the open Atlantic. I wonder if she will be seasick.

For the first few minutes she was alone at the big round table, until an elderly couple came to join her. It was a silent meal, for after introducing themselves, the newcomers said nothing more to her and spoke only monosyllables to each other. It was only at the end, when she was sampling the cheese and fruit, that Kay appeared with the fifth occupant of their table. He was a middle-aged man, spare, conservatively dressed, with short-cut grey hair and rimless glasses—unattached, Philippa decided at a glance, well-to-do, used to ship travel and to catering to his own whims without concern for any dependents. Kay introduced him as William Harris. She had met him in the bar, she said casually. Philippa, exchanging a few polite phrases, shortly left the table. Glancing back as she went out of the diningroom, she saw the elderly couple still silently finishing their meal and Kay talking animatedly to an attentive Harris.

Philippa sat for a while in one of the public rooms where a program of piano music and singing was offered for the staider passengers. It was still early when she returned to the stateroom, eager to go to bed and read for a while in peace and solitude. She found the stateroom full of evidences of Kay's preparations for the evening. The top of the dressing table now held bottles and jars of cosmetics. Garments hung over the backs of the two chairs. The bathroom was still steamy from the shower and damp towels hung from the shower stall. The fragrance of the roses was lost in the stronger scent of soap and bath salts. At least, thought Philippa, she doesn't favor perfume.

She got into the bed away from the portholes. Kay's bathrobe and the paperback books were still on the other. As she sank back against the piled-up pillows and opened her novel she luxuriated in the sense of catered-for comfort, the fresh, clean sheets, the good, strong reading lamp, above all the privacy. This was what she had looked forward to after the discomforts of a working vacation spent in rugged surroundings. She wondered how late Kay would be in coming to bed. Harris seemed scarcely the sort who would fit into Kay's world. But there was never any telling how even a man so set in his ways might be seduced by someone like Kay. If she wanted him. No doubt he would be a stepping stone, a means of meeting other men. She wondered why she was so certain that this was Kay's intent. That was it. Kay had said, somewhere along in their conversation, that she was at a loose end. There seemed to be a hiatus in her regular occupation. Perhaps there was also one in her personal involvements. But why, Philippa abruptly asked herself, am I so concerned about her? She certainly has her way of life and I have mine. All we have to do is keep off each other's necks for the next five days.

She read for an hour or so and then, growing drowsy, laid the book aside and sought sleep. The motion of the vessel was much more marked. Occasionally there would be a long roll from side to side that awakened creaking sounds in the stateroom. The steward had come in before Philippa had returned and had closed the portholes once more. She was confronted by another dilemma. It seemed churlish to turn out all the lights in the stateroom and leave Kay to stumble about in the dark. It might also be unwise. Between the motion of the ship and the amount of liquor Kay undoubtedly had had—She is certainly used to a great deal more than I am. Will she, in fact, be able to find her way back here? And I suppose she will remember she doesn't have the stateroom to herself and bring somebody back with her. It will be awkward if she does forget and I have to turn him out. If she comes in the worse for wear, will she remember that both the stateroom and the bathroom have raised sills, high ship sills? If she trips over them, she'll go sprawling.

Philippa brought herself up short. Why do I have to go worrying over her like this? She's not my responsibility. In the end, Philippa left the lamp on in the bathroom and the door ajar and turned her back on the bar of light that fell across the room.

Nevertheless, in spite of her resolve to think no more of Kay, she could not sleep soundly. Every so often she came to the surface of consciousness and wondered vaguely where Kay was and what she was doing, before drifting back into sleep. Once she turned her bedside lamp on and looked at her watch. Midnight. She lay for a while feeling the long roll of the ship and listening to the creaks and rattles in the vessel. Occasionally a spray of white water flashed at the portholes. They must be well into the gale. Eventually the rolling motion lulled her back to sleep.

She did not know what time it was when the sound of the door opening awakened her. She saw Kay's silhouette against the light in the passage before the door closed again. She heard Kay curse under her breath.

"I'm awake," Philippa said and at once turned on her bedside lamp.

Kay said thickly, "I was wondering if I was in the right place. The door wasn't locked."

"I left it unlocked. I did not know whether you had your key."

Kay stood uncertainly in the middle of the floor. She stared at Philippa. As the ship rolled deeply toward the ocean side of the stateroom, the spray of a great wave dashed against the glass of the porthole, hissing as it passed. Kay made a desperate attempt to cling to the wardrobe but lost her footing and fell heavily over Philippa.

"Good God! How long is this going on?" she mumbled into Philippa's ear.

"I don't know." Philippa gently pushed her away until she sat upright on the edge of the bed. "From the weather forecast it looks as if we'll have a stormy crossing."

Kay looked at her with fear showing in her eyes. "Will it get worse?"

"Perhaps," said Philippa matter-of-factly.

"But isn't this dangerous? It feels as if we could turn right over. Haven't ships done that?"

Philippa smiled in spite of herself. "Well, not very often. And not modern liners like this one."

Kay got up, clinging to the wardrobe, and staggered towards the bathroom. At least, thought Philippa, she is not seasick, even with all that whiskey.

Philippa picked up her novel and tried to focus on what she was reading. But her eyes kept straying to watch Kay. Kay pulled off her dress and kicked off her slippers. She went into the bathroom, stumbling slightly over the high sill. Philippa waited tensely for the sound of a fall but none came. Presently Kay emerged wearing only her bra. She is as slim as a teenage girl, thought Philippa, staring in spite of herself at Kay's narrow pelvis, long legs, the tuft of fair hair at her pubis. Kay, oblivious of her gaze, rummaged unsteadily in one of her bags, lying open still unpacked on the floor. She pulled out a shorty nightgown and, dropping off her bra, pulled it over her head. Her small, softly hanging breasts were hardly more than those of an adolescent girl. Carefully Kay found her way around Philippa's bed and into the one under the portholes, pushing the books and robe off onto the floor. She answered with a mumble when Philippa said goodnight and turned off the lamp.

Philippa lay wakeful, listening to the sounds of the storm. Within moments Kay was asleep, snoring lightly. Well, thought Philippa, for a while she will not be aware of the storm. Gradually the noises of the storm merged into a symphony of sound and Philippa once more fell asleep.

She was awakened by Kay stumbling past her bed to the bathroom. The light by the other bed was on and by it she saw Kay struggle against the upward roll of the floor. Involuntarily she called out, "Be careful of the sill!" and cringed to hear the sound of the fall that this time she thought must be inevitable.

But her warning had been in time and the sound she heard was Kay retching. So it has been too much for her—the motion and the alcohol. Goodness! Her whole stomach must be coming up. Philippa waited watchfully till she heard the taps turned on in the washbasin. After a few minutes Kay came out of the bathroom and staggered weakly across the room. Philippa moved over on her bed and Kay, as if she recognized this slight movement as an invitation, sat down on the edge. She was very pale and her hair was wet where she had splashed water in washing herself. Her eyes were red-rimmed and unhappy.

"I expect you should have taken the dramamine after all," said Philippa gently.

"I'm sorry. I think I need a little scotch."

"Do you have some?"

"It's in my other bag," said Kay but she made no move to get up.

Philippa got out of bed on the other side and, steadying herself carefully against the roll of the ship, found the bag lying on the floor of the wardrobe and sought in it for the whiskey bottle. She poured some into a glass and held it for Kay to drink.

"You'd better get back into bed now," she said, putting her hand under Kay's arm to guide her back to the other bed. Kay docilely obeyed her and Philippa covered her firmly with the bed clothes.

The next morning the ship was alive with sound. In the growing daylight they could see the great white-capped waves race past the

portholes. The windows in the diningroom, Philippa found when
she arrived for breakfast, were half-boarded up. She had left Kay
in bed, sleeping heavily. After breakfast she went to watch the
storm from the shelter of the enclosed deck and then sat for a
while in the library, reading a magazine. But about ten o'clock she
told herself that she could no longer procrastinate. She must go
and find Trudy.

Trudy saw her the moment she stepped into the tourist lounge.
"Oh, come over here, Phil! Isn't this storm wild?"

She led Philippa to a corner where they could sit together on a
leather-covered sofa, away from the cooped-up children and their
parents.

"How is Lawrence?" Philippa asked.

Trudy laughed. "Lawrence refuses to admit he is seasick. But he
couldn't eat breakfast and he doesn't want to get up. I see it hasn't
got you down. It never does, does it?"

"No. I just couldn't sleep soundly."

"Did your roommate keep you awake? How is she doing?"

"She was upset. It is her first sea trip. It's too bad."

"Her first? I wonder why somebody like that would cross the
Atlantic by ship. Has she told you?"

"Of course not. Why should she? I suppose she thought it
would be enjoyable."

Trudy was watching her closely. "I wonder how you are going
to make out with her. She seems to drink a lot. You didn't see the
crowd that came aboard with her at Southampton, did you?"

Philippa answered guardedly, "I saw a group that I've since
realized must have been aboard to see her off."

"Well, my dear! What a noisy bunch they were! I've felt sorry
for you ever since I found out she was your roommate. She is not
your type at all, Phil."

"They are just theater people."

"Theater people! Movie people. That's worse. You know, when
you introduced me I thought her name was a little familiar. I went
and looked up the passenger list. She had something to do with
producing that film that made such a commotion last year when it
was nominated for an award. You remember, the Student Union
wanted to bring it to Deerfield but the board of trustees refused to
allow it. Though I must say, when Lawrence and I saw it later I
didn't think it all that scandalous—no more sex and nudity than is
usual these days. It was a very good film, really. Did she tell you

what she does?"

"She is a film editor. It seems she is beginning to make a name for herself."

"Well, I hope she doesn't make your trip too uncomfortable."

"There is no reason why she should. She is very considerate, really."

"No bad habits as a roommate?"

"None that I have noticed so far," Philippa declared stubbornly.

Trudy was still watching her as if she did not believe what she said. But recognizing what she saw in Philippa's face, she merely answered. "Well, it's early days, Phil. I hope you won't have to change your mind."

Philippa saw very little of Kay during the rest of the day. She stayed away from the stateroom till nearly lunchtime, supposing that Kay would want to sleep to make up for the troubled night. When she did go down to get ready for lunch she found Kay sitting up in bed, rubbing her eyes and running her hands through her tousled hair.

"The wind must have died down a little," Philippa said cheerfully. "There is less motion."

Kay said pessimistically, "I don't see much difference." She paused as another big wave slapped against the porthole over her head and then said plaintively, "Is it going on like this for the rest of the trip?"

Philippa, watching her wan face, said with compassion, "It is hard to say how long this sort of weather will last in the north Atlantic. But you'll get used to it. Why don't you come and see if you can eat some lunch?"

"A drink is more what I need."

"Didn't you have more than enough last night?"

The tone of her voice brought Kay's eyes to her face. "That's right. You gave me some last night, didn't you?" There was open mockery in her manner.

Philippa flushed faintly. "You asked me to get it for you."

Damn! thought Kay. I have hurt her feelings and I really don't want to. What a hangover I've got! Or am I seasick? Aloud Kay said, "I don't think I can face food without a shot of scotch." She got out of bed and went and rummaged in her bag for the bottle Philippa had replaced. Straightening up she looked directly at Philippa and asked, "Have a drink?" Seeing the No beginning to take shape on Philippa's face, she added crossly, "Come on, have a snort. It won't kill you."

She fished ice-cubes out of the ice-bucket on the dressing-table and put them into two glasses and poured whiskey on top of them.

Reluctantly Philippa took the glass she was handed. She stood with it in her hand until Kay impatiently demanded, "Come on. Drink up, and I'll go to lunch with you."

Obediently Philippa took a sip. Kay took a swallow and set her glass down while she went to the bathroom and bathed. Philippa sat down in the one armchair and waited. Presently Kay came out of the bathroom naked and began to dress.

Kay said, "I'm sorry I woke you up last night. But I was scared blue. Just my luck. The one and only time I go to sea it has to storm."

"You're fortunate it doesn't affect you more than this."

Kay paused in brushing her hair to look around at her. "You are really an optimist, aren't you?"

Philippa answered before she could stop herself, "Do you object to a cheerful outlook?"

"Oh, my, no! All right. I'm sorry again. I didn't mean to be smart. I suppose it's nice to try and look on the bright side. I ought to try it some more."

Philippa studied her pointedly. "Is it so difficult?"

Kay glanced at her again. "Right now it is, for me."

Philippa's vexation melted. "I'm sorry. You had not mentioned that you had any special reason for being unhappy."

Kay was suddenly belligerant. "What makes you think I have?"

Philippa, surprised, said, "Why, that was the implication of what you've just been saying."

Kay examined her face suspiciously. Reassured, she said, "I thought you were needling me."

"That is something I'm not likely to do."

"Oh, now, don't get uptight again! Yes, I'm edgy. I came on this ship to get away from the people I've been with for the last two months. I'm just feeling anti-social, I guess. And besides, they like to pry into your private affairs. I thought if I went home this way there would be five days when I wouldn't run into any of them."

Philippa thought, isn't that what I'm doing? Aloud she said, "Sometimes one needs to be off by oneself."

"Well, at least if not by yourself, with a different crowd.

Especially if your private life isn't going right."

Man trouble, thought Philippa. Aloud she said, "Shall we go to lunch?"

Kay agreed and they left the stateroom. When they arrived in the diningroom they found they had their table to themselves. The windows were still half-shuttered and Kay gave them an apprehensive glance. Philippa, noticing it, said comfortingly, "Don't think about them."

Kay gave a little laugh. "If it is something you don't like, ignore it. Well, I'll try." She picked up the menu and for a while they spoke only of the food.

When the steward had brought the first course and moved away again to his station, Kay said, "The trouble is, I haven't any sort of backbone at all. I'm swayed by everybody. Especially somebody who says he is in love with me. He tells me he will kill himself unless I go to bed with him. And I find myself doing just that. Then he says, we've had a nice time, haven't we, but I've got to leave now. What would you do in that situation?"

"I don't think I would have got into it in the first place."

"No, I don't suppose you would have. You're probably in much better control of your life than I am of mine."

"Our circumstances are no doubt different." Philippa's tone was neutral.

Kay shot her an amused glance. "No doubt," she mimicked. Her mind reverted to her own problems. "But suppose it isn't like that, after all. He does love you but he has to leave. You won't hear from him again until he can arrange his personal affairs. The trouble is he has a wife and she won't let him go."

"Why do you bother with him, then?"

"Because I love him. I can't give him up."

The bitterness in her voice caused Philippa to look up from her plate. "I still think it would be the path of wisdom to part company with him."

"The path of wisdom! What's wisdom got to do with it?" Kay's eyes and voice were angry. "You don't love somebody because you choose to do so! Love isn't something you can measure out! Or is that all you know about loving somebody? If so, you haven't a clue to what it's all about."

Wildly Kay's inner debate carried her beyond awareness of Philippa seated opposite. Of course, she assured herself, I know he does not like writing letters, personal letters, and I did get those two from him after he left Paris. It was that last week we were together when he got so upset. He was going to a new assignment, he said, in Latin America. It was going to be a difficult job. He couldn't talk to his wife about us right now, he said. He would have enough on his hands in his professional life. His wife was necessary for that. He would have to maintain appearances till this crisis was over.

In the midst of his soothing phrases she had realized that he was returning to his wife willingly and even eagerly. And in the heightening of her sensitivity at the approach of their separation Kay had been acutely aware that, during that last week, his attentiveness to her had lessened. He absently overlooked her preferences about things. He was impatient with her demands on his time. When she had protested he had been contrite, telling her that he was beside himself with anxiety about the problems of his new assignment. She admitted it was unreasonable for her to tax him so. Of course he was harassed. A woman like herself, with a professional life of her own, must surely be able to understand the pressure he was under, and that their personal life would be temporarily affected.

Philippa's voice came to her in the midst of this welter of many times rehearsed self-debate. "This certainly does not seem to be a very good subject for us to discuss."

Oh, God! thought Kay. She is angry. What did I say? She acts as if I insulted her. Aloud Kay said anxiously, "Forget it, do. I shouldn't talk so much about myself." She paused, drinking nervously from the water glass, and looked at Philippa's stern face. She added humbly, "It's just that I'm really so miserable." Now why do I have to go and grovel to her? Kay demanded indignantly of herself. There she sits, like virtue personified, wishing she could get rid of me.

But Philippa said gently, "Perhaps things won't be so bad when you get home." Philippa thought, she must have interrupted her job for him. She must be trying to join him in spite of the fact that he has gone back to his wife. What a wretched business.

Kay said, "Don't worry. I'm not going to spend the rest of the trip crying on your shoulder."

Philippa turned aside to let the steward place the second course before her. She waited until Kay had been served and the man had withdrawn before she said, "If it eases your feelings, please do. Since I am a stranger, you need not feel constraint."

Her cool voice, the delicate choice of words struck on Kay's heated feelings like drops of cold water. A stranger, a useful confidante. But she said, "I don't feel you are a stranger now," and then added quickly at the faint surprise that showed on Philippa's face, "Oh, don't mind me!"

She was surprised when Philippa suddenly smiled and said, "I don't mind at all."

The rest of the time they were together they talked carefully of impersonal things, about Rome, about London. After lunch they parted and Philippa saw nothing more of Kay until late that evening. Then she glimpsed her in the nightclub, seated next to a man wearing a brightly colored jacket, with several large-stoned rings on his fingers. She hasn't lost much time in finding a solace for her misery, thought Philippa.

Their second day out the weather improved. There were gleams of sunlight that turned the great heaving grey billows blue for short periods of time. In the evening the sky was clear enough for an uncertain sunset. Streaky clouds, fitfully brilliant, gave a respite from the stormy gloom, but it was a false hope of fair weather. The wind dropped but it still battered at anything that could flap or dangle.

Philippa spent a large part of the morning in the library and in the afternoon she went to the movies, more out of a wish to avoid the need to listen to Trudy. Now and then she came upon Kay. She was always accompanied by a man, a ship's officer or another passenger. Whoever it was, he was obviously intrigued by her. She is a very pretty girl, thought Philippa. Perhaps too thin and always nervously smoking a cigarette. But vivacious, talkative and with a lightning fast response to any situation. She was an erratic but energetic ping-pong player. Philippa stood and watched her play on the enclosed games deck, running laughing to catch the ball when the motion of the ship added complications to the play. She was also a very good dancer. For a short while before going down to the stateroom for the night Philippa sat in the nightclub and watched her dance in the spotlighted dance floor with several different partners.

It was again very late when she arrived back in the stateroom. Philippa, wakeful, watched her undress and stumble into bed. She was still sleeping soundly when Philippa left the stateroom next morning to go to breakfast.

At ten o'clock Philippa went down to the tourist class lounge.

She must not neglect Trudy, whose husband was also on the faculty at Deerfield College. Trudy was on the alert for her. She was seated comfortably where she could watch the doorway and continue her energetic knitting.

"Oh, Phil! I wondered where you were. Have you been having trouble with your roommate?"

"Why, no. Why should you think so?"

"Well, she is getting downright notorious."

"Notorious?"

Trudy smiled at her brightly. "Oh, you know what I mean. In the first place, she drinks like a fish. It seems she is the last to leave the bar when it closes and even then the bartender has to turn her out. Doesn't she disturb you when she comes in? Or doesn't she sleep there at all? As a matter of fact, I heard that last night she finished up in someone else's stateroom—a man's, of course. Was that true?"

"It is not. Kay came back to our stateroom. She is sleeping there now."

Trudy gave her an inquisitive glance. "Did you notice what time she arrived there? She probably visited somebody before turning in."

Philippa paused to control her temper before she said, "Trudy, where do you hear all this sort of thing? I'm sure you are repeating what someone else told you, because you and Lawrence don't spend the night in bars."

"Oh, you know how it is, Philippa. Lawrence has made friends with some of the younger ship's officers. The young fellows, you know, like to talk about the women on board—who is an easy lay and who isn't. Vulgar, isn't it? But that's the way they talk. There isn't any doubt about what they think about your roommate. And I don't think she cares what they say about her. Of all the people for you to have share a stateroom with!"

"Kay gives me no trouble at all."

Trudy laughed. "Well, I can see how that would be. She is scarcely under foot at all, is she? So long as she doesn't bring her boyfriends back with her or expect you to like that sort of company." There was a gleam of malice in Trudy's eyes.

They were interrupted by Lawrence, who came and sat next to his wife. "Hi, Phil. Haven't been bothered by the rough weather, have you?"

"It never does, you know," Philippa said equably.

Trudy said to her husband, "I was telling Phil about her roommate's doings."

Lawrence, a saturnine man with a long nose, grinned. "Quite a girl, from what I've heard. The modern type. She's some sort of scenario writer for the movies—you know, one of those hundreds of names they flash on the screen at the end of a film. Some people I've talked to even recognized who she is."

Trudy said, "Well, I suppose we should take all this sort of thing for granted. People in the movie world seem to live at a different pace from ours. She believes in making friends, all right. That young fellow in the purser's office—what is his name, Lawrence? He is up on everybody aboardship. He says that she started out with that tall, middle-aged man who sits at the same table with you, Phil. What is his name?"

Philippa said guardedly, "William Harris."

Trudy said, "He must have turned out to be too staid for her. He probably couldn't stand her drinking."

Philippa said, "He is very conservative."

Trudy said, "More your type, Phil. I hear he is a pretty wealthy man—unattached and just the right age."

Philippa, recognizing a fixed idea of Trudy's, said, "Indeed. He is pleasant company. But I think he would be boring."

"Phil, you can't be so exacting."

"Why not, Trudy? I haven't the slightest interest in getting married."

"Well, you should—" Trudy began, but Lawrence, aware of Philippa's annoyance, broke in with,

"Well, your roommate, Phil, isn't so conservative. She likes her men on the livelier side. Trudy, you know that man who wears loud jackets and sports all those diamonds? He is a speculator of some sort. He's the fellow she spent the night with."

"She did not," Philippa declared, before she could stop herself.

Lawrence glanced at her in surprise. "You don't say?"

Trudy with a malicious little smile, said, "Phil says she was a good girl and came right home to bed."

Philippa, aware that she was flushing, said quickly, "You've been listening to a lot of gossip, Lawrence."

Lawrence and Trudy exchanged glances and he said, "Oh, no doubt, no doubt. You know how it is on shipboard. It's a means of entertainment. But you might let your friend know how she is talked about. Or isn't she that type?"

Philippa ignored his question. As soon as she could she left them and went to the writing room to answer the letters she had picked up in London. But she found it hard to concentrate. It was silly, she admitted, for her to spring so vehemently to Kay's defense. It seemed beyond question that Kay was ready and willing to sleep with casual acquaintances. Nor did Kay seem to give much importance to doing so. Probably she would not care in the least if she knew about the gossip that was being circulated about her.

Kay did not appear at lunchtime. Philippa began her meal alone but soon after she was joined by Harris. He was gravely polite. He had, he said, spent part of the summer in Florence. He often did this, he said. He found it a renewal of the spirit to spend a couple of months each year amidst the glories of the Renaissance, whether in Italy or further north in Europe.

Philippa, listening with practiced attention, thought, he must be almost sixty years old and his tastes certainly were completely formed before the second World War. It was just as well that Kay was not present. But then, if she had been, Harris would probably not have been so talkative, so ready to expose his outlook on things to her derision.

He asked urbanely, "You go abroad frequently?"

"Not every year. This time I was on a study grant."

"Your subject is—?"

"I am a philologist," said Philippa. "I have been interested for some time in the linguistic remnants of the classical languages in eastern Europe."

He hesitated for a moment before saying, "Indeed. I have never thought of that possibility." He seemed to savor the novelty of the idea.

Philippa reflected that she knew his type very well. He was a man, like many who had inhabited her parents' world when she was a child—reserved, highly educated, with low-keyed emotions, given to cultivating a patron's interest in the arts, in carefully calculated proportion to the financial means at his disposal. Of course Trudy would think him a suitable husband for her. In Trudy's eyes she was his female counterpart. And yet she rebelled at this assumption. She denied to herself that her feelings were really so cool, so controlled to the point of negation. She knew her blood could run hotly sometimes. It was for lack of stimulus, lack of a congenial attraction. Yet by now she was almost forced to admit that, not having found that attraction at nearly forty years of age, she could scarcely expect it to appear. She paused in her thought. Perhaps that was it. Her emotions were really only responsive to the subtly right appeal. Whereas Kay's, quicker and more constantly in use, responded instantly to any attraction.

She became aware that Harris had gone on talking and that she had no idea what he was talking about. She disguised her lapse long enough to pick up once more the topic of his conversation and finished lunch with him in amicable ease.

As the afternoon wore on the weather again grew rougher. The great ship was in mid-Altantic now and moving into the path of another, fiercer gale. Many passengers, as if made uneasy by the increasing motion, wandered restlessly about the enclosed deck and the public rooms. In mid-afternoon Philippa, seeking exercise by walking on the comparatively sheltered side of the upper deck, came upon Trudy, her head tightly swathed in a large kerchief. They walked up and down together a few times, battling the wind and the rolling of the ship, shouting their remarks to each other to be heard above the noise of the gale. Lawrence, said Trudy, was in the card room, playing chess with someone he had met. Finally she asked, "Couldn't we go down to your stateroom, Phil?"

Her curiosity knows no bounds, thought Philippa. Reluctantly she replied, "Why, yes," and led the way indoors, wondering if Kay was up and dressed.

They plunged into the warm shelter of the amidships lounge and found their way down the deeply carpeted stairway and along the narrow, white-walled corridor to the stateroom. At the door Philippa paused and gave the panel a sharp rap as she put the key in the lock.

"Goodness! It's after three. Surely she's up by now!" Trudy exclaimed as Philippa opened the door and they stepped into the empty room. "Or did you think she might have a visitor?"

Philippa said nothing. Trudy sniffed the air. There was a mingled scent of stale cigarette smoke and bath salts. Philippa's bed was made up but Kay's was open and tumbled. The stewardess had quickly learned to come in after Philippa left for breakfast and tidy the room while Kay slept on, rolled up in the bedclothes, oblivious to noise.

But Kay's garments were strewn about as she had left them when she had finally got up and dressed. Trudy at once spotted the shorty nightgown cast down on Philippa's bed, the pantsuit

Kay had taken from the wardrobe and then discarded and left hanging over the one armchair.

"She's pretty careless, isn't she? How do you stand it, Phil? You're so neat yourself."

Philippa picked up the nightgown and tossed it onto Kay's bed. Then she gathered up the pantsuit and hung it in the wardrobe. All she said was, "Sit down, Trudy. I'll call the steward to bring us some tea."

She rang and gave the steward their order. As they waited Trudy said, "You're certainly traveling in style, Phil. Though I must say this is pretty cramped for two people who don't know each other. I'm really amazed at you. I never would have thought that you could adapt to living with anybody. In fact, I've always thought that was the real reason you never got married—you couldn't stand the untidiness."

Philippa was silent for a moment. She thought, I've been hearing remarks like that from Trudy for years. She knows she offends me when she says them but she can't resist. She really means that she doesn't think I can stand the idea of having sex—that the sexual act is too messy for me. I'm a freak of nature. Philippa said aloud, "After all, it is the stewardess who has to put up with that."

The steward brought the tea tray into the stateroom and placed it carefully on the dressing table, compensating with his bodily movements for the motion of the ship. His sharp eye saw the tumbler that had been used for whiskey and he picked it up to carry it away. Trudy also saw it.

"She even drinks here, I see," she said.

Again Philippa ignored the comment. After a moment she spoke of Harris and his talk about Florence. She regretted her choice of subject at once as Trudy pounced on it.

"He is a little old for you but he is certainly well-heeled. You've got a decided taste for luxury, Phil. He could certainly supply you with a lot."

Philippa said, annoyed, "Trudy, he is not in the least interested in marrying. He is unattached because that is the way he likes to live. He wants to move about as and when he pleases, without a woman to cause complications. And you know that I am not in the market."

"You are not in the market because nobody has aroused your interest. But that is something you have to cultivate, Phil. Oh, well, he is probably one of these disguised misogynists who cover up their dislike of women with a preoccupation with culture. Oh, I know the type."

"Let's talk about something else, Trudy," said Philippa and finally led her away from the subject.

By the time dinner was over that evening it was evident that the storm had engulfed the ship. The stewards had lashed down all the movable objects and several passengers had lost their footing in staggering about. The elderly couple did not appear at the table but Harris came to join Philippa. He gazed about the almost empty diningroom and said, "I trust Miss Stephens is not ill."

"I don't know. I have not seen her today."

"She shares your stateroom, does she not?"

Philippa nodded and waited for him to make a further comment, but he did not. Then she reflected that his silence said perhaps more than any remark such a reserved man would be apt to make.

All at once he got to his feet and Philippa realized that Kay had come up behind her. Kay seemed surprised at his formality but sat down quickly and began to talk about the casualties of the storm.

"Even the ship's officers say this is unusual." The whiskey she had been drinking in the bar made her flushed and animated. But even so, in the subdued light of the diningroom, thought Philippa, she looks much younger than she is.

"You're fortunate not to be affected by the rough weather, Miss Stephens," said Harris.

Kay gave him a glance from under her lashes. "No, I'm not seasick. But I am a bit scared." She flashed a sudden smile across at Philippa. "I'd be scared out of my wits if I had to spend the night alone in the stateroom. Philippa is very reassuring. Somehow I don't think the ship will go down with her."

She talked on, gay, uninhibited, heedless of Philippa's taciturnity and Harris' stiffness. But even Harris, Philippa noticed, began to unbend under the barrage of her chatter, though several times he blinked in shock at the forthrightness of some statement she made. Philippa was aware that, in the half-gloomy ambience of the diningroom, their table was an oasis of cheerfulness that even the stewards noticed.

Kay left them after two courses. Philippa sat on, nibbling at cheese and fruit, while Harris finished his meal. Though he said nothing more about Kay, it was apparent to Philippa that the impression she had made lingered on. Afterwards he went with Philippa to the ballroom for the evening's entertainment, sparsely attended because of the violent motion.

There was no sign of Kay when Philippa returned to the stateroom. She got ready for bed and tried to settle down to read for a while. But she found herself restless and uneasy. Why? she wondered, since bad weather at sea never upset her. She wondered if Kay had gone on to the cabaret show in the nightclub with someone—perhaps the shady character that Lawrence Dimock had described, of whom she had had a glimpse the evening before. Or whether Kay was sitting in the bar drinking, alone or with a chance-met companion. And if she would be able to get back to the stateroom safely. People had been known to break arms and legs in weather like this.

She broke off her thoughts in vexation. Good Heavens! Why am I worrying about her like this? She is really no concern of mine. I am not responsible for her simply because she shares my stateroom. She set herself purposefully to forget Kay. But again and again she found her thoughts had strayed from the page she was trying to read. This is ridiculous, she told herself finally, and glanced at the clock. Only 11 o'clock. Far too early to expect Kay. As she was thinking this, a key turned in the lock and Kay opened the door and stepped over the sill.

"Hello," said Kay briefly, reaching desperately for support as the ship plunged wildly.

"Hello." Philippa was about to add something further but a glance at Kay's face changed her mind. She remained discreetly silent as Kay sat down in the armchair and kicked off her slippers.

"Yes, I'm early," Kay said, answering her unspoken remark. "It's not much fun trying to dance if you're likely to be stood on your head."

"I'm sorry—"

"You needn't be. There's nothing you could do about it."

Her tone was so ill-natured that Philippa fell silent again and took up her paperback novel. Kay lit a cigarette and sat smoking, her legs stretched out and her ankles crossed. Philippa, glancing covertly at her, saw that she was brooding.

Kay suddenly spoke. "It's the same thing, every single last damn time. And every time I say I'm not going to do it. I'm not going to give anybody—and I mean anybody—a chance to try it on with me. And every time I'm in the middle of it before I know it."

Philippa waited for a moment and then asked, hesitantly, "In the middle of what?"

"Of the sex scene. Maybe I just attract that type. I meet a man and all he does is try to get me into bed with him before I know what's going on—if not sooner."

The fellow in the loud jackets with the diamonds, thought Philippa. But she said nothing.

"I'm not a kid any more. I used to think it a joke—you know, go out with a guy and end up in bed with him. You'd find out a lot about a guy in a hurry that way. But, damn it, I'm tired of all that now. I've got some serious things on my mind but nobody seems to be interested in that. The only people I meet seem to be somebody who wants another body in bed."

In spite of herself the distaste she felt showed on Philippa's face. Seeing it, Kay stopped abruptly and demanded, "Why are you looking at me like that? It can't be any news to you that I have sex whenever I feel like it—with anybody I choose to. I'm sure your friends have told you all about me."

"My friends?"

Kay gave a bitter laugh. "Gossip goes both ways, doesn't it? Go ahead. Own up. You've heard talk about me."

"Yes. I discount it."

"Kind of you. Why?"

"I never take for granted the accuracy of what someone says about someone else."

"Oh, you don't? Well, what have they been saying?"

Philippa thought, I thought you knew. But aloud she said, "That you drink a good deal and pick up a good many male acquaintances."

Kay was silent for a while. Finally she said, in a different tone of voice. "I haven't been drunk once all summer. I haven't been to bed with anybody but one man. I didn't need to. I'm not making my name in my profession by sleeping around with influential people. I didn't need liquor to give me enthusiasm for what I was doing. I didn't have to drink to drown despair." She stopped and smoked abstractedly.

"One does not need such—distractions when one is content with what one is doing," said Philippa carefully.

Kay's glance was satirical. "No, one doesn't," she mocked. There was another silence and then she said, once more bad-tempered, "Besides, what's so wonderful about a woman like me doing what she pleases? I've been doing it since I was in my teens."

"I realise that girls nowadays have changed their attitudes to such things. But they still stir up gossip when they behave so—uninhibitedly. I know that from some of my own students."

"Don't you remember your own college days?"

"Yes, but they have no application here."

Kay studied her face. "Where did you go to college?"

When Philippa named the state university she had attended, Kay seemed to speculate. "I don't know much about the social climate there. Where I went you learned how to shed your parents' hang-ups pretty fast—if you hadn't already liberated yourself in high school."

"Liberated yourself?"

"Freed yourself from all the quirky notions about sex you grew up with."

"Oh. But that would only be if you found your parents' notions untenable."

"Well, didn't you?"

"No. I agreed with my parents' ideas generally. I always thought my parents were quite rational people. They treated me as a rational being."

"Dear me!" Kay mocked. "You mean to say you took everything they said about everything as gospel, even your sex life?"

"I wasn't concerned about my sex life when I went to college. That wasn't what I was there for."

Kay stared at her for a long moment. As she did so her expression changed from goodhumored derision to open contempt. "Do you mean to tell me you are a virgin?"

The slight color rose slowly in Philippa's face. "It's just as honorable a state as yours." Her voice was instantly a thin, sharp whip.

Kay's eyes glowed as she jeered. "You're certainly a case of retarded development. I'm simply amazed somebody hasn't laughed you out of it. It's ridiculous for a woman of your age in this day and time. Papa and mamma kept you pure?"

Philippa was so angry that for a few moments she could not speak. She did not even hear Kay's further remarks as she reasoned herself back into equanimity. Finally she said, cutting into Kay's statements, "You're quite mistaken. Of course it used to be that a decent woman had no choice but to be a virgin unless she married, if she wanted to remain respectable. But one does have a choice now and I made a different one from yours—and from that of most of my friends."

The cold evenness of her tone registered with Kay. The derision in her face and voice faded. She said grudgingly, "Well, you can call it a choice, I suppose. But it's more likely inhibitions or cowardice. And are you still tending the vestal flame?"

Anger rose again in a choking wave in Philippa's throat but she checked it by saying abruptly, "It seems to me preferable to follow one's own inclinations when it comes to the disposal of one's body. I was never convinced of the need for being persuaded to go to bed with someone simply to prove I am not peculiar. I think I have been more content than some of my friends who followed your sort of advice. It doesn't look to me as if you're very happy about having sex with anybody and everybody just to satisfy a physical appetite. I think you are trying to convince yourself that you enjoy something you don't really want."

Kay looked away to avoid Philippa's direct gaze. Philippa went on, "You're the one who is afraid—who is unsure of herself—who thinks she needs to prove something to herself or to someone else. Or are you paying back someone you think has made use of you and deserted you?"

She stopped as Kay got up without speaking and walked to the bathroom and closed the door. Dismay swept aside Philippa's indignation. Dear God! she thought. What have I done now? She is angry and we have two more days to get through before we reach New York and can escape each other. How could I have done such a stupid thing—let my feelings carry me away like that? But it is years since anyone has affected me as intensely as she does.

She sat tense, still pretending to read, listening for sounds from the bathroom. She supposed that in due course Kay would come out, silent and resentful, and that they would begin the business of watchfully ignoring each other. Even if Kay had provoked the situation, she should have swallowed her feelings.

The bathroom door opened, much sooner than she expected, and Kay stepped back into the room. She had taken off her dress and stood in her panties and bra. She said, as she reached into the wardrobe to hang up the dress, "Well, maybe you've got a point there." The tone of her voice indicated that she had spent the few minutes in the bathroom mulling over their conversation and had decided to ignore the last of Philippa's words. She did not seem angry or resentful but simply preoccupied by their interchange.

Philippa, in grateful relief, said warmly, "I'm sorry, Kay, if I spoke too hastily. I didn't mean—"

Kay cut her short. "If you didn't mean it, you shouldn't have said it. You're just playing games." There was resentment in her voice now. "When you spoke you sounded as if you meant what you said."

"I couldn't have meant it more," said Philippa, goaded into frankness again. Then she relented and added, "But plain speaking is not always suitable."

Kay said with a sly smile, "Suitability as the measure of honesty."

She will not provoke me this time, Philippa told herself. But Kay had seen the flush rise in her face again. "Don't pay any attention to me. I'm in a foul humor. That's no excuse and I shouldn't take it out on you. But you're so available, aren't you? You can't get away from me. Unless I go and find somebody else to sleep with."

"That's hardly necessary." Philippa's tone was crisp.

Kay gave her another glance full of unspoken humorous comment. But her expression almost at once changed and she was absorbed again in the inner debate. It was no use running away. She always seemed to meet herself around the next corner. Philippa was right. It solved nothing, this frantic bed-hopping. It was more than ten years ago that she had first had sex. She could remember distinctly the chagrin, the disappointment, the unhappiness she had felt after that first act, with a man who had been surprised and half-angry to find her a virgin and who had avoided her ever afterwards. She had listened to all the arguments and been persuaded that they were true—that sexual intercourse was liberating, mind-freeing, fulfilling, the supreme pleasure. She had not found it so, but had not dared to state openly what she really felt. I suppose, she thought, glancing furtively at Philippa's calm face as she sat once more reading, she has always been too stiff-necked to make that mistake. And now what am I doing—running away from a situation that gives me too much pain for me to reconcile myself to it. This is only temporary, she told herself once more. It's only until he can get things straightened out. He does love me. It is weak of me to doubt him simply because he is trying to act sensibly.

She looked up to find Philippa gazing at her with concern. "Are you all right, Kay?"

"Yes, of course. I told you, I'm in a bad humor. I just hate everybody and especially these men I'm always getting entangled with. Don't the men you go out with ever want you to finish the evening in bed with them?"

"The first time, perhaps, they may expect it. But not the second."

"If there is a second time," said Kay skeptically.

"There sometimes is. If not, it doesn't worry me."

"You probably like solitude more than I do. Don't you think sometimes you might be missing something?"

"No. I've never felt a lack. It would be quite different, I am sure, if I met someone I liked very much."

"So that's it. You just don't like people."

Philippa retorted sharply, "I did not say so. I imagine I am not as gregarious as you."

"Now, now, don't get all upset again. I'm just talking."

"I'm not upset, but I don't like to have words put in my mouth."

"I won't do it again, I promise," Kay said lightly. "Hell. As a matter of fact, I wish I had some of your starch. Then I wouldn't go to bed with a man just so as not to have the trouble of turning him down."

"But why do so? What compels you?"

"Yes, what does? Well, I didn't tonight and I'm wondering why the hell I didn't, why I pushed that guy in the face. I don't like him much but he was entitled to think I was expecting to go to bed with him. I gave him every reason to think so. He's furious." She laughed wrily. "It must be some time since a girl ran out on him and left him half way up." She made a suggestive gesture.

To cover her own embarrassment, Philippa asked, "Well, why did you?"

Kay was silent so long that Philippa wondered if she would reply. She said slowly at last, "Because I thought of someone else."

She turned away and began to take off her panties and bra and walked about the stateroom naked, clutching at support when the heavy rolling of the ship paused abruptly in a lurch. She is too thin, thought Philippa, but she is beautifully made and her skin is like satin. Philippa's eyes dwelt on Kay's breasts, soft, pink

nippled. Suddenly aware of her own response to the sight she
looked quickly away.

She said aloud, "Is it someone who has made you unhappy?"

Kay said, "I've told you about him. He's married, he has a
career job that means more to him than anything else, he has gone
to a new assignment, he has written me two letters in three weeks
and I write him practically every day. I won't be seeing him when
I get to New York. I'll just be waiting there the way I've been
waiting in London—"

The promise of tears in her voice grew so strong that she was
forced to stop speaking to keep them from overflowing.

"In that case," said Philippa, "I don't see that anything you do
with someone else is any concern of his. Aren't you upsetting
yourself needlessly?"

Kay, slipping a nightgown over her head, said sulkily, "It's easy
enough to be cool and collected about somebody else's feelings. I
love him. And he does love me. It's just this separation that makes
me doubt him."

She dropped down on the edge of Philippa's bed and leaned her
head on Philippa's shoulder. "I'm so tired of the whole business. If
I could just forget him for a while, at any rate."

Philippa, acutely conscious of her warmth against her breast,
patted her head. "We can't all discipline our emotions. Perhaps
none of us can at all times, at least. Brooding does make us see
things out of proportion. See if you can't go to sleep and forget all
about it for a while."

Obediently Kay straightened up and moved over to her own
bed. They exchanged good nights and Philippa put out her reading
lamp. In the noisy dark of the storm she listened for sounds from
the other bed but there were none. She lay awake for some time,
aware with all her senses of the girl lying near her.

By morning the weather had grown calmer again. Kay woke
while Philippa was in the midst of dressing but she seemed too
drowsy to talk connectedly. By the time Philippa left the
stateroom to go to breakfast she was once more asleep.

When Philippa returned to the stateroom in the middle of the
morning Kay was gone and the stewardess was there making the
beds. Miss Stephens, she said, had got up and dressed half an hour
before.

There was a stir about the ship that Philippa recognized as the
effect of approaching land. They would disembark in New York

the following morning just after breakfast. That fact and the
quieting of the storm created a sense of excitement among the
passengers. Harris, with whom she had breakfast, and the Dimocks
when she saw them later, all commented on this change of
atmosphere.

"I wonder," said Trudy as they sat together for a mid-morning
cup of broth in the tourist class lounge, "if your roommate will
have as noisy a welcoming party as the one that saw her off in
Southampton."

"She may be being met. She has a lot of friends on both sides of
the Atlantic."

"She has? You've learned something about her, haven't you,
Phil? Anything interesting?"

"Yes, she's an interesting person. No, nothing personal—except
her professional life. I never knew before anything about
filmmaking. I've learned quite a bit."

"Oh, Phil! There you go—being deaf, dumb and blind where
people's private lives are concerned! Haven't you found out
anything about her love life?"

"No," said Philippa blandly, and thought, at least I've learned
how to lie.

Trudy stared at her speculatively. "I don't believe you." But
Philippa persisted and in the end Trudy changed the subject.

Shortly after she left Trudy and went on deck for a bit of
exercise before lunch. The wind was not so strong and there were
sheltered corners where she could sit and enjoy the few gleams of
sunlight that found their way through the wracks of cloud. In one
of these nooks Philippa came upon Kay, wrapped in a tweed coat,
brooding glumly out at the grey, heaving water. At Philippa's
startled, Hi! she looked up and said, "Oh, hello."

There was another chair beside her and Philippa dropped onto
it. "This doesn't feel exactly like Bermuda weather, does it?"

"No. Is that where we are now?"

"We're near."

Kay thought, I'd know her anywhere, by that cool, quiet voice.
She talks like a schoolteacher, but there is something lurking
under that precise manner. She really has elegance—that tall, slim
body, that long-legged walk, but with the knees held in, not a
stride. I used to despise all that sort of thing in a woman. I used to
think it meant an inhibited, narrow-minded, bloodless sort of
bitch. What the hell has she done to me that makes me see

something else? When she turns her head to look at me she doesn't
seem cold at all, but warm, welcoming, welcoming me, seeing me
as me. Oh, hell! It is the grey-blue eyes that look out at you from
that classic face, with its deep eye-sockets, straight nose and
narrow chin. She has a complexion like porcelain.

Philippa's voice interrupted her. "Have you been gambling on
the ship's run, Kay? There is a big pool being made up for the last
twenty-four hours' run. It seems there is just enough promise of
fair weather to make the guessing tricky."

"Oh, I bet on the first day, but nothing came of it and I forgot
about it. By the way, have you got a nickname? Philippa is rather
a mouthful."

Philippa's laugh was gay. "People call me Phil."

"Phil sounds like a boy. I wouldn't think of you as a boy."

"Well—" Philippa stopped, as if thinking better of what she was
about to say.

Kay saw her hesitation. "Go on. Say what you were going to
say. Don't be so cautious. I won't make fun of you." There she
goes again, thought Kay, seeing the faint color come into
Philippa's face. She added suddenly, irrelevantly, "Tell me what
your other nickname is."

Philippa still hesitated but under Kay's gaze finally said, "My
mother called me Pippa—after Robert Browning, you know."

"Yes, I know." Kay's eyes sparkled mockingly. "Guess what? I
had Browning in college, too. 'The year's at the spring, And the
day's at the morn,' ta ta ta, 'God's in his heaven—All's right with
the world.' What a crashing bore he could be!"

Philippa said equably, more interested than offended, "I take it
you were not very fond of Browning."

"I liked Elizabeth better. But even she—I suppose you have to
be fair. Some of these things would be a lot more effective if they
were not quoted to death. Take Christina Rosetti. Everybody
knows, 'My heart is like a singing bird, Whose nest is in a watered
shoot.' But I like the second stanza better—

" 'Raise me a dais of silk and down,
Hang it with vair and purple dies;
Carve it in doves and pomergranates
And peacocks with a hundred eyes;
Work it in gold and silver grapes,
In leaves and silver fleur-de-lys;
Because the birthday of my life

Is come, my love has come to me.'
You know, that imagery has always conjured up all sorts of things." Kay paused for a moment and then glanced back at her. "And I even know what vair means."

Philippa smiled at her indulgently. "You do? I expect Christina was thinking of a mediaeval tapestry, full of ladies with long swanlike necks, dressed in gowns with trailing sleeves trimmed with squirrel fur—vair, that is—"

"In gardens with peacocks and grape arbors, surrounded by walls with espaliered fruit trees," Kay finished for her.

They exchanged smiles. Philippa said, "You recite poetry very well."

"I used to learn a lot of poetry by heart. I still do, when I find something I like. Once, in my first year in college, I thought I wanted to be an actress."

"You changed your mind."

"Yes. What I am doing now is much more—gripping. It seems to me more creative—" Kay suddenly broke off and Philippa saw that she was looking up at someone standing near them.

Philippa turned and saw that it was Trudy, muffled in a shapeless coat, with a woolen scarf wrapped around her head. Trudy giggled. "Don't tell the captain I'm out of bounds." As she spoke her eyes, bright, inquisitive, were fixed on Kay.

Obediently, Philippa said, "Trudy, you remember this is my roommate, Kay Stephens. It's nice to be able to be out on deck, isn't it, Trudy?"

Kay's manner was so noncommittal when she replied to Trudy's greeting that Philippa thought, she is going to get up and leave, just when we were beginning to enjoy ourselves.

Trudy was saying, "Aren't you the Kay Stephens who did the editing on the film version of *The Suburbanite*? It was a candidate for the year's ten best, wasn't it?" She talked on glibly, energetically. Philippa thought, she has been researching the subject. She must have been expecting to waylay Kay. And of course Kay sees that that is what she has been doing, preparing for this moment.

Kay's answers were monosyllabic, unenlightening. But she made no move to go. Philippa, encouraged, joined in the conversation, seeking to deflect the full effect of Trudy's barrage of words. Just as she began to despair, the sound of the mealtime gong reached them faintly.

Philippa, gambling, said, "That is the first call for lunch and I am hungry. Shall we go down to lunch together, Kay?" Absurdly, her heart beat faster as she waited for Kay's reply.

Kay, with surprise, said, "All right. I didn't have any breakfast." Trudy, looking from one to the other, said brightly, "Lawrence is always starving. I'd better go and find him."

I'll hear more of this later, thought Philippa, the next time Trudy gets me alone. She glanced at Kay but Kay seemed to forget Trudy the moment they left her. They were alone at the table. Half of the time, as they ate, Kay talked earnestly or satirically of her summer in Europe, and half the time she was mute and preoccupied. Occasionally, after a longer than usual silence, she looked across at Philippa and said wrily, "You haven't got a very gay lunch mate, have you?" or "Don't sit there looking so understanding. Give me a kick in the pants. It might liven things up." When Philippa retorted, "Don't be silly," Kay laughed and said, "You know, I'm going to miss you. Nobody has cut me down to size this way for a long time."

They went back to the stateroom together after lunch, Philippa with the idea of doing some packing, certain that Kay would seek other company. But instead Kay threw herself down on Philippa's bed and lay staring at the sky through the porthole. Philippa, standing in front of the wardrobe, reached in to sort out her clothes. Several times now she had found Kay's dresses and pantsuits thrust carelessly in among her own things. She drew out a mini-skirted silk frock and moved it down to Kay's end of the wardrobe. If Kay had ever been taught tidy habits as a child, she had completely abandoned them as an adult.

As she moved about the stateroom she glanced now and then at Kay, lying silently on the bed. It was obvious that a cloud had come over the cheerful mood that she had shown through lunch. No doubt, Philippa thought compassionately, the approach of land and the prospect of whatever normal life ashore might hold for her was absorbing her now. Philippa remembered Kay's statements about the man with whom she was involved. It was a pity that a girl like Kay should allow herself to be made use of by someone as self-centered as that. But perhaps it was inevitable that such a girl should do just that—be the natural victim of a man's demands. Perhaps it was as inevitable a role for her as Philippa's austerity was natural to herself.

Kay's voice startled her. "What are you thinking about?"

"You," Philippa said without hesitation.

"Me!" Kay raised her head from the pillow to stare at her.

"Yes, you. I do sometimes think of people—or a person—and not always of abstract problems."

"Don't speer at me." There was mild reproof in Kay's tone. "But why should you be thinking about me?"

After a short silence Philippa said, "Because I like you and I'm sorry that you're unhappy."

Kay raised herself on her elbow. "Who said I was unhappy?"

"You did."

"I? Oh, last night—" She left the sentence in the air. She sat up and swung her legs off the bed. "Would you like to go to the movies? It's a comedy. I've seen it before but I could see it again."

Philippa, surprised, said Yes. When they came out of the theater it was late afternoon and they sat on the enclosed deck and had a scotch together, watching the clouds part for a colorful sunset. Their talk was easy, desultory, companionable. It seemed natural then that they should return to the stateroom together to dress and go down to the captain's farewell cocktail party. At dinner afterwards they found themselves at table with the elderly couple and Harris. Their comfortable comradeship slowly dissipated in the more general talk. By the end of dinner Philippa noticed that Kay was once more restless and quick-tempered. She finally took leave of them all with a careless, "See you again sometime," with an extra glance at Philippa.

Philippa spent the rest of the evening with Harris, conscious of a letdown, an acute boredom in listening to his studied, slow-spoken small talk. She saw no sign of Kay and guessed that she had retreated to one of the bars. Just before going back to the stateroom she went in search of the Dimocks. It behooved her to preserve good relations with Trudy for the sake of peace during the college winter.

She found Trudy in a strategic corner of the tourist class lounge, cheerful and talkative from watching the pre-disembarkation activities of her fellow passengers. And at first it seemed that this immediate entertainment would prevent Trudy from speaking of Kay. But very soon Trudy said,

"This is your last night to put up with your roommate. Tomorrow you'll be home in your own nice peaceful apartment. I still don't see why you wanted to come first class. You'd have been spared putting up with her."

Philippa tried not to show her vexation. "I might have done worse in tourist—probably sharing with two or three others instead of one. Besides, I haven't had anything to complain of in Kay."

"Really? That seems hardly possible, from what I've heard. She's pretty promiscuous."

"She's nothing of the sort!"

"Dear me, Phil. Don't get so het up. If she's not, she is pretty careless of appearances."

Philippa, vexed with herself at so openly betraying her feelings, said firmly, "Trudy, we all lead very staid lives. I do, in any case. I imagine that if I were in Kay's world I'd behave rather differently."

Trudy laughed merrily. "Why, Phil, you couldn't possibly be anyone but yourself no matter where you were!"

"That's as may be," Philippa said, still annoyed. "I don't want to discuss her. You know very well, Trudy, that I don't like to gossip about people. What is said is usually quite erroneous."

"Oh, have it your way, Phil. But I've never known you to get so defensive about anybody before."

Philippa got up abruptly and said, "Well, good night, Trudy. If I don't see you in the morning, I'll be in Deerfield tomorrow evening."

Still ruffled, she went down to the stateroom to finish her packing. She looked around at Kay's things still strewn about the room, her dresses and pantsuits still hanging in the wardrobe, her suitcases still tucked away empty in a corner. She hoped Kay would remember to leave herself a few moments for packing. The steward had warned them that all their luggage would be required, packed and locked, ready for the porters the next morning at seven-thirty. Finally she got undressed and got into bed.

The sixth time she roused from a light sleep and looked at her bedside clock it was four o'clock and Kay's bed was still empty.

"She has forgotten about her luggage," said Philippa, speaking aloud in her anxiety.

She gave up the effort to seek sleep again and left the light on, lying on her back gazing at the ceiling. In less than half an hour she heard sounds in the narrow, short corridor outside the stateroom door. Someone was bumping against the wall and cursing in a low voice. She got out of bed and unlocked the door and peered out. Kay stood leaning against the jamb, searching unsteadily in her small handbag for her key. Philippa reached out to guide her inside.

Or tried to. Kay stumbled over the high sill and fell full-length on the stateroom floor. There was now little motion to the ship, so her failure to keep her balance was not due to the unsteadiness of the floor. Besides, thought Philippa, she reeks. She leaned over and shook Kay's shoulder. "Kay, have you hurt yourself? Kay, get up. Get up and get into bed."

Kay's response was mumbled and incoherent. She tried to shake off Philippa's hand. Obviously she wanted to be left where she was.

Philippa said firmly, "No. You can't spend the rest of the night on the floor. Get up, I tell you." She reached under Kay's arms and pulled her bodily to her feet. Half dragging, half lifting her, she got her over to the bed under the portholes. At first Kay rebelled but then yielded to her efforts. The moment she lay down she was sound asleep.

Philippa shook her again. "Kay, wake up and take your clothes off." But Kay's only answer was an incomprehensible mutter. She turned over and relapsed into sleep. Philippa gazed down at her for a moment, watching the transformation caused by deep sleep. Kay looked much younger, more vulnerable. Philippa began to undo the zipper of her dress, unhook her bra, draw off her panties. Kay did not stir, even as she tucked the bed clothes around her.

When she had finished she paused before going back to her own bed and gazed out of the porthole. The presence of the sea outside was more felt than seen. But every so often a crest of white water raced past, reflecting light from the ship. In the silent blackness they seemed to be speeding towards their destination with an extra burst of speed to make up for the stormy hours in mid-ocean.

When she woke again it was half past six and already there were sounds in the ship of a stir and bustle. Philippa glanced at her own bags. They were packed and ready. Only her overnight case was still open to receive her last minute things.

She looked across at the other bed. Kay lay as she had last seen her, motionless in a deep slumber. After a debate with herself, Philippa decided to leave her alone for a while longer.

She got up and dressed and went out on deck with the first daylight. The ship was already inside the Narrows, going slowly through the grey, oily looking water, past familiar landmarks.

"Good morning," said Harris' voice at her elbow. She replied to his greeting and they stood together at the rail or walked about to catch glimpses of other vessels or buildings ashore becoming slowly more distinct in the increasing light. Finally he suggested breakfast. It was already past seven-thirty. Philippa thought, surely the stewardess will have waked Kay by now and perhaps will help her to pack. I am sure Kay won't want breakfast.

By the time she had finished breakfast the ship's public rooms and corridors were full of people milling about amid piles of luggage. Giving in to her sense of anxiety, Philippa went quickly down to the stateroom. The door was locked. When she opened it and stepped in she saw at once that her own bags had been removed. But Kay still slept and her clothes still hung in the wardrobe or lay where she had tossed them over the furniture. If the stewardess roused her, thought Philippa, she must have gone back to sleep at once.

She stepped over to the further bed and shook Kay.

"Wake up!" she said urgently. "You've got only half an hour to get ready! Kay, wake up! We're in New York harbor! We're about to go ashore!"

Kay stirred and tried to shake off her hand. But she persisted and finally roused the sleep-drugged girl to get out of bed and go into the bathroom. Then she stood irresolutely staring at the clothes hanging in the wardrobe. There was a knock at the door and the stewardess opened it and put her head in. The woman frowned at the littered room and said severely, "I'm sorry, ma'am, but you must be out in fifteen minutes."

"I'm ready," said Philippa. "You have my bags already. But Miss Stephens has overslept."

The stewardess said defensively, "I woke her an hour ago. She said she would get up at once. Dear me, none of her things are ready."

"I'll see if I can help her get them together," said Philippa.

The stewardess withdrew, saying disapprovingly that Immigration was already checking passengers in the forward lounge.

Philippa knocked on the bathroom door. "Kay, you must hurry. We've got to get your things packed."

Kay opened the door and stood looking at her groggily. Her eyes were red-rimmed and bloodshot and there was a smell of stale whiskey about her. She looked down at herself and asked irrelevantly, "Did I go to bed raw?"

Philippa snapped impatiently, "It was as much as I could do to get your clothes off. I didn't think a nightgown mattered."

Kay gave an unsteady laugh. "No, I don't suppose it does."

Philippa said peremptorily, "Kay, get under the shower. I've got some eyedrops you can use. Shall I see if the stewardess has something for a hang-over?"

Kay, still standing unsteadily in the middle of the bathroom, said feebly, "It would just make me sick."

"Well, get in the shower. I'll begin to pack your things."

As Kay got into the shower Philippa began to pull the clothes out of the wardrobe and off the hangers. She was half-finished when Kay came out, still toweling herself.

"What are you going to put on, Kay?"

Kay pointed to a red wool pantsuit. She dressed hastily and fell to helping Philippa pack her second suitcase.

"No, no!" Philippa exclaimed, seeing her cram clothes in by main force. "You'll never get everything in that way." She snatched the garments from Kay's hands and quickly folded and rolled and fitted until she had the case full. Twice the stewardess came to urge them on. At last everything was packed away and the bags stood locked in the center of the floor. Philippa methodically opened all the drawers of the dressing table to glance into them once more. When she turned away from this task, satisfied, she found Kay standing close to her with a small smile on her lips.

"Thank you very much, Pippa. I'd have gone ashore all bits and pieces without you."

"I should have awakened you earlier. But I thought the stewardess would see to it."

"I expect she thought she had." Kay's tone was apologetic.

Bells were ringing and there was the sound of heavy movement in the ship. But they still stood confronting each other, suddenly reluctant to part.

Kay said in a soft voice, her eyes troubled, "I've been a nuisance, haven't I, Pippa? You're probably glad to see the last of me."

Philippa smiled, shaking her head. "I shall miss you, Kay." Then she spoke more formally, "Are you being met?"

Kay laughed derisively. "Do you think any of the goons I associate with ever get up at this hour in the morning?" She added more soberly, "Are you stopping off in New York?"

"No. I'm going straight on to Deerfield."

"That is where you teach?"

"Yes."

"Well, I'm not likely ever to be in Deerfield." Kay's face grew sober. Philippa saw her shiver, as if some superstitious dread had seized her for an instant. "I don't like goodbyes."

Philippa, eager to seem cheerful, said lightly, "Oh, we'll probably come across each other some time. You know where you can address a letter to me."

"I practically never write letters. And there is no use my giving you an address because I'm never in one place for very long. I expect this is it."

Well, yes, thought Philippa. There is no reason why we should ever meet again. This is just one of those brief interludes of travel. Under the impulse of this feeling she placed her hands on Kay's arms and gazed at her compassionately. Kay stood passively, dejectedly. Philippa, eager to comfort her, said impetuously, "Oh, Kit-Kat, don't let people lead you where you don't want to go!"

Kay instantly stiffened under her grip. She drew back in order to look into her face. "What did you call me?"

Philippa, confused and daunted by her abrupt response, was tongue-tied. They stood looking at each other in silence till Philippa dropped her hands and they slowly turned away from each other. Neither of them said anything more, beyond a few commonplace remarks about the luggage, the immigration formalities, the disembarkation operations. The last time they saw each other was when Philippa, stepping off the gangway, saw Kay go in search of the bay in the huge landing shed where her bags would be placed. They waved to each other across a sea of people.

PART II

It was unaccountably odd to be back in her normal surroundings. Usually, when she returned from a summer's absence to her apartment in a building at the edge of the campus, there was a feeling of comfortable familiarity. There was a certain sense of ease at picking up small daily habits again. Really, she supposed, she felt most at home when she was alone and absorbed in the details of her professional life. Her apartment afforded her the undisturbed orderliness in which she was most relaxed, free to give her attention to the scholarly pursuits that interested her. Any interruptions of this intellectual calm came at scheduled and predictable times—the hours she spent in classrooms and seminars, with students or fellow faculty members, or with friends with whom she mingled in a more or less fixed pattern of small dinners, concerts, theater parties.

But this time she was aware of a sense of uneasiness. It was as if there was still unfinished business that hovered just over the horizon. She found herself, in the midst of dealing with her normal concerns, half abstracted, as if she were on the watch for some half-expected interruption, as if she were listening for the telephone or waiting for some other communication from outside this quiet, familiar routine. She tried to shake off this strange feeling of expectancy, this undercurrent of restlessness. She had never been restless like this before when she had returned from travel.

She lived in a pleasant garden court building which gave the illusion of a house with a garden, surrounded by trees, shrubs and plants. Living alone for so long she had acquired fixed habits, and she had come to dislike any interference with them. She resolutely tried to reestablish them, getting her own breakfast, tidying the slight disorder of the living room, making her bed. These were all things she did not do when traveling and she enjoyed the contrast.

But now, as she dusted briefly in the room she used as a study, she found her mind straying constantly to the voyage home and the short, intimate interlude of her life aboard with Kay. Again and again she found herself dwelling on some detail of their moments together, on some phrase or statement of Kay's. After the hundredth time of catching herself doing this she thought, with annoyance, it was just because I've never done anything like that before; it was the only time I've ever had to share day-to-day living with a stranger like that. Whenever, in traveling, she had before this been forced to share a room with someone else, a discreet wall had always remained up between herself and the other woman, a wall that had been carefully maintained by both of them. It was Kay that had demolished it—Kay who had behaved as if no such barrier existed.

She found herself remembering Kay in sudden vivid glimpses— Kay in a mini-skirted dinner dress with her long hair caught up in a swirl on top of her head, standing naked in the bathroom brushing her teeth or rummaging in the wardrobe for a change of clothes. Or Kay talking about herself when they were alone, or at the dinner table, running circles around Harris's deliberate, ponderous speech. And most of all the last time they had stood together in the stateroom, in the end wordless. There had been no barrier at all between them at that moment.

The third morning after her return, as this recollection once more came vividly before her mind's eye, she stopped herself with a final angry flick of the dustcloth and went impatiently to get her handbag and jacket. It was almost ten o'clock and this was the day of the weekly meeting in the faculty lounge of the members of her department. Her eyes fell on the morning's paper, still in a tight roll on the side table by the front door. That was a measure of the collapse of her normal routine. She had dawdled too long in this pointless woolgathering to leave herself time to scan the paper. She was reminded that she had not even listened to the early morning news report on the radio. Well, she might as well glance at the headlines on her way across the campus.

She closed her door, making sure it locked. As she walked slowly down the path that led across the still green expanse to the building in which the faculty lounge was located, she unfolded the paper. Large headlines stared up at her: U.S. diplomat kidnapped by guerrillas. Another kidnapping, she thought, and glanced down the column to pick up the details. What she read made her stop and stand still in surprise. The newspaper account said: Stafford Price, a career foreign service officer recently accredited to a Latin American government, was waylaid and abducted by a group of terrorists on a road on the outskirts of the capital. It went on to describe what was known of the kidnapping and stated that the armed men were members of a radical group in opposition to the regime in power. Price had been spirited away to an unknown destination. No further details were yet available and no ransom demand had yet been received. Word from the abductors was awaited before any action could be taken either by the U.S. or by the local government.

Philippa slowly resumed her walk across the campus under the almost leafless trees. Stafford Price, her cousin Elaine's husband. As she walked she studied the large photograph of Price. She recognized it as a picture that had been taken two or three years ago. It showed a handsome man about thirty-five, blonde, clean-shaven, smilingly self-confident. Stafford had always had that air of self-confidence, based on the fact that his good looks, his easy, urbane manners, his ability to make use of other people's knowledge, had always paved the way for his social and professional success. Philippa wondered now how he would manage in this situation. None of those talents would be likely to be of much use with terrorists.

Then she reproached herself. This was after all a pretty cool way to look at it. Stafford might be in great danger. In fact, it could easily be that he had already been killed by his kidnappers. She turned her thoughts to his wife, her first cousin. Elaine was her only living close relative. That fact gave her a certain value that had nothing to do with their personal relationship. As children they had been companions, not because of any great liking for each other, but because their families lived close together. Their parents thought, since they were of an age and both only children, there should be a close bond between them. There never was, except the bond of mutual antipathy, thinly disguised by a sense of solidarity in the face of parental pressure. They had grown up with different temperaments, tastes, and desires. By the time they reached their teens and their lives diverged they had ceased to have any real communication. By now their intercourse was limited to Christmas cards and birthday remembrances and an occasional letter or postcard when one of them traveled abroad.

Nevertheless they were first cousins in a family that had always put emphasis on the dutiful recognition of its members by each other. Philippa wondered if she should call Elaine by long distance. There was really nothing she could do except express sympathy, offer moral support. She was reluctant to do so. Elaine was surrounded by official and unofficial sympathizers, people far

more able to support and comfort her. She knew that Elaine was
still in Washington. One of the letters that had awaited her when
she returned to Deerfield was one saying that Elaine's mother was
incurably ill. "I couldn't go with Stafford to Paris," Elaine had
said. "Mamma has been failing very much. Now I think I have
found a comfortable home for her and that means I can join
Stafford in a month or so. I had hoped to go with him to his new
post, but that wasn't possible. I shall still be here in Washington
when you get back from abroad. I don't intend to give up the
apartment. It is too convenient for when I need to come back
here."

Philippa, when she had first read the letter, had recognized the
authoritative, positive tone that was so much Elaine's and which
she had always found so irritating. Elaine was a wealthy woman.
One of the differences that had set them off from each other was
the fact that Elaine's father had been a well-to-do business
executive, while Philippa's parents had only their joint income as
teachers and scholars. To give her her due, Elaine had never made
a question of the difference in their financial status. But the
consciousness of inheriting a good deal of money gave her an air of
command even in her personal relationships.

However, thought Philippa now, that isn't something I should
hold against her now. She is probably frantic over Stafford.

When Philippa entered the lounge the first person she saw was
Trudy Dimock. Trudy was a faculty wife but she was so active in
college affairs that she was more often in evidence than her
husband.

Now she said, pouncing on Philippa, "Have you been in touch
with your cousin? What's the inside story, Phil?"

Philippa held up the paper she had been reading. "I've just seen
the news."

"Why, Phil! Didn't you hear it on the early news program? I
know you listen to that regularly."

"Not this morning. I haven't fallen into my usual routine yet. I
know nothing about this, Trudy, except what it says here."

"Well, then, you'll have to call Elaine right away."

Philippa noted the familiar "Elaine". Trudy had never met
Elaine and Philippa was surprised that she had remembered who
Stafford Price's wife was. But no, she wasn't surprised. It was the
sort of thing Trudy remembered—that Philippa had a cousin who
was the wife of a minor official in the U.S. government whose

name occasionally appeared in the newspapers.

"Well, I can't call her right now, Trudy. Perhaps after the faculty meeting. Besides—"

"Besides what?"

"I haven't made up my mind whether or not to call her. I can't be of any use and it is a nuisance to have people call you up in a crisis like this, just to say a lot of meaningless words."

"Oh, don't be so stand-offish, Phil! Of course she will want to hear from you—probably is counting on it."

Philippa thought, you just can't wait for me to talk to her so that I can give you all the details, can you, Trudy? Aloud she said, "I don't think I will call her. I'll wait for her to call me. If she really wants me, I'll hear from her."

The news in the evening papers and on television was full of Stafford Price's kidnapping. His abductors had been heard from. They demanded several hundred thousand dollars and also the release from prison of various members of their group. Stafford would not be harmed if their demands were met. But any attempt at retaliation would result in his execution.

Philippa, eating a light supper off a tray in her study, listened to the broadcast thoughtfully. How would Elaine take this? She would undoubtedly be outraged, indignant. But would these feelings obscure her concern for him as her husband? Philippa had wondered sometimes during the ten years since their marriage just how they felt towards each other. Oh, yes, Elaine was possessive. Possessiveness was her most outstanding trait, in all her dealings with other people. If she did not wish to possess you, then you knew that your value in her eyes was rated very low. She had always been extremely possessive of Stafford. And Stafford had always shown himself as highly appreciative of his well-off, socially prominent wife. But there was a fluidity about Stafford's character, a suppleness, a readiness to conform to the demands of the moment. She knew Elaine was aware of this. She suspected that Elaine had known it before the wedding, in which Philippa had been her bridesmaid. There had been one or two unguarded moments when Elaine had shown her rage, bitter disappointment, grief over Stafford's blithe behavior.

There were those, Philippa remembered, who believed that Elaine had married Stafford, somewhat against his will. But these people overlooked the fact that Stafford appreciated fully the advantages of being Elaine's husband—and even, thought Philippa,

counted on Elaine's rigidity, her unswerving belief in her own
dominance, to protect him from his own follies.

The morning news had little to add. There had been conferences
between U.S. officials and those of the local government about the
payment of the ransom and the freeing of the political prisoners.
No clue had been found to Stafford's whereabouts. It was known
that he had been spirited away to a remote part of the country, a
region of wild, desert mountains almost inaccessible even to army
units.

In spite of her resolve not to call Elaine, Philippa found herself
on the alert. She avoided Trudy. Even though she tried to ignore
the radio and the television, she found herself listening carefully to
the noon broadcast. There had been an airplane highjacking and
the kidnapping was temporarily eclipsed by this more recent
outrage. In the evening, when she returned to her apartment after
a fully occupied afternoon, she found the evening paper on her
doorstep with a wide black headline: Mystery woman enters Price
case. Philippa, dropping her handbag on the hall table, sank into
the nearest chair and read the item. A young woman who refused
to reveal her identity had informed news reporters that she had
spent a good deal of the past summer in Paris with Price and that
she knew he had had dealings with the radical group that now held
him hostage. She said that she was ready to cooperate with U.S.
officials, provided her own safety was assured. The newspaper
story went on to the effect that no information was obtainable
about the young woman, who was attractive and whose exact
relationship to Price was not clear. Philippa, reading this
statement, wondered how much more clear it needed to be made.
Obviously Stafford, in Paris without Elaine, had been having an
affair.

Philippa put the paper down and was about to get up when the
phone rang. She was not really surprised to hear Elaine's voice,
peremptory, saying without preamble, "Philippa, you must come
to me. I need you."

"Yes, I will come, Elaine, if you really do need me. But are you
sure? I'm only just back, you know."

Elaine cut her short. "You must come. There is no one else I
can ask to help me. I cannot tell you the circumstances on the
phone. I shall explain when you get here. When you hear what I
have to say, you will understand. There is a plane—"

Philippa impatiently interrupted. "Yes, of course, I will come if you really need me. But it must be in the morning, Elaine. I shall have to make arrangements here for someone to take over my classes for me. No, I cannot come tonight. Tomorrow, then, yes, tomorrow."

Getting off the plane at the National Airport at noon next day Philippa was still pondering the essential question. Of course it must have something to do with Stafford's summer in Paris. The morning news had had further details about the mystery woman. She now threatened to tell her story directly to the news media if government officials refused to listen to her. State Department officers admitted that they were embarrassed by her threat of revelations. What had Stafford Price been doing while in Paris? This question was carefully evaded.

But why, Philippa asked herself as the cab took her up Connecticut Avenue, if it is something to do with Stafford, must she have me to help her? Her encounters with Elaine had been few since the wedding and the number of times she had talked to Stafford could be counted on the fingers of one hand. Elaine had always given the impression that her life was, in every detail, just what she planned it to be, that she was in command of all the forces contained in it. Philippa was certainly not a necessary element in it—except, perhaps, as background—the learned cousin who contributed to the distinction of her family's intellectual tradition.

This speculation is all pointless, Philippa thought as the cab arrived at the large apartment house set in elaborately landscaped grounds. I won't know until she tells me. A chill wind scraped dried oak leaves along the pavement at her feet as she stood beside the cab waiting for her change. Elaine had said that there would be a government agent in plain clothes on guard in the lobby of the building and another at her own door. They would be warned of Philippa's coming.

Elaine herself opened the door of the apartment and drew her inside, leaning forward automatically to give her a perfunctory kiss.

"Tom Reidy from the Department has just left," she said. "He wanted to wait till you got here, but he had to leave."

"Why does he want to talk to me?" Philippa asked, bewildered.

"He wanted to ask you whether you had seen Stafford in Paris this summer. I told him that I was positive that you had not. I did not want him to stay till you got here. I want to talk to you alone.

I'll call down to the receptionist and tell her to take messages, if anybody else comes or calls me on the phone. You've no idea how maddening it is to fend off reporters and busybodies. Come. I've put you in the spare bedroom."

She picked up Philippa's bag and walked across the big livingroom. The mirror at the end of the short hall reflected them as they approached—Elaine's taller, larger, dark-haired image contrasting with Philippa's fair slenderness.

Elaine put the bag down on the bedroom floor. "The maid can take care of your things, Philippa. Come into my room. What I have to say must be strictly private."

She led Philippa across the hall to her own big bedroom, situated in the corner of the building, so that it had windows in two directions. As she closed the door she said,

"I asked you to come because there is something I can speak of only to you. There is no one else who can help me."

Philippa, surprised and uneasy at her manner, said hesitantly, "I would have thought, Elaine, that there are many other people who could be of more use to you."

"Not in this matter." For a while Elaine said nothing further and Philippa waited in silence. Presently, Elaine said,

"You must have seen the news stories about this dreadful woman and what she says about Stafford."

"There is something about someone referred to as a mystery woman, who says she knew Stafford in Paris during the summer."

"Yes, that is it."

"Has she anything to say that is of consequence?"

Elaine suddenly burst out impatiently. "She is making a lot of irresponsible statements in the press! But that is not what concerns me now. Philippa—"

Elaine stopped and Philippa, unused to hesitation in her, watched her warily. Elaine bit her lip and her hands opened and closed nervously on each other. Her eyes, when she glanced at Philippa, were stormy.

Elaine started speaking again. "It seems incredible to me—I cannot believe it, even now."

"Believe what?"

"Believe that Stafford would willingly have done such a thing—would contemplate doing such a thing."

Impatiently Philippa said, "Elaine, the news account says that a woman has come forward to say that she saw a lot of Stafford in

Paris this past summer and that she knows he had dealings with these people who have now kidnapped him. Is that what you cannot believe?"

"I don't know whether that is true or not. Stafford was in Paris on a confidential mission. He did not tell me what it was when he went. Tom Reidy says he cannot tell me about it now. It involves U.S. security. No, no. I don't know anything about that. As for what she claims about herself and Stafford—I suppose that can be refuted. She is probably a blackmailer, a sensation seeker, somebody who thinks she can make money out of these so-called revelations."

Elaine was speaking rapidly, contemptuously, as if she wanted to clear away these nonessentials to get down to important matters. Typically Elaine, thought Philippa. "Well, then, if you are not so concerned about that, why have you sent for me?"

Elaine did not answer for a while. Then she said, "Philippa, when they first told me that Stafford had been kidnapped, I was incredulous. He had only just left me, here in Washington. He arrived in Ciudad Nueva one day and late the evening of the next he was abducted. I had just talked to him on the phone a few hours before. Nobody could understand why he was the victim of this plot, at first. It was supposed that he wasn't really picked out to be the victim. It just happened that he was a newly arrived U.S. diplomat and happened to be where it was easy to kidnap him. But when the news got back here Tom Reidy began to suspect that it had something to do with what Stafford had been doing in Paris. So he asked me to go through the letters Stafford wrote to me. I did. There was nothing useful in them. Stafford was very discreet about that sort of thing."

Elaine paused and Philippa saw that her nervousness had increased, that she was having difficulty speaking clearly.

Elaine went on. "I was distrait, Philippa, thinking of Stafford and what might be happening to him. I went through his personal things. He had left a drawer full of letters and other papers. I—I found several letters written on that thin paper the English use, in envelopes with English stamps, addressed to him from London, sent to a club here he belongs to."

She stopped and Philippa waited silently while she mastered herself.

"They were from a woman—are from a woman, I should say. She writes to him as her lover and refers to being with him in

Paris. But more than that. She reminds him that he said he was coming home to tell me that he wanted a divorce so that he could marry her."

When she stopped again, Philippa thought, oh, Lord, she is going to break down! What do I do now?

But apparently Elaine had got over the first shock of grief when she had first read the letters. Rage possessed her now. "What a fool she is! She makes quite a lot of comments about me, referring to discussions they had had together—" Elaine frowned angrily at the recollection. "I suppose he did not defend me. He must have let her think he agreed with her. Stafford is so soft, especially with women. He lets them believe anything they want to rather than be forthright."

Philippa, surprised at this candor, looked at her curiously. She said aloud, "But do you need to believe what this woman says?"

Elaine turned to look at her directly. "In public I shall deny everything she says."

"In public?"

"In public." Elaine seemed to lose patience. "Can't you see, Philippa? I know that what this woman says is essentially true. Don't you see that what she is threatening to disclose will include all this business between herself and Stafford? And don't you realize that I know that Stafford was probably swayed by her for a while? This is not the first time Stafford has become involved with a woman. He is like wax in any woman's hands—up to a point. I have confronted him with this sort of thing before this. It was a shock to come upon these letters. But I am thankful that I saw them before this woman came forward in the news. It has given me time to think what I should do. In her letters she says they were lovers—that the time they spent together in Paris was a love idyll. I'm not so blind that I don't see that Stafford must have acquiesced in that." Elaine paused again and her eyes shone with a bright, vindictive light. "You can see from her letters how she was chasing him—saying that he had promised her that as soon as he got back to Washington he would tell me that our marriage had ceased to exist. If she thinks that Stafford would do that, she is very much mistaken. I have no intention of giving him a divorce."

"But, Elaine, what if he obtains one without your consent? Did he say anything about this when he came back from Paris?"

"Not a word, of course. Do you think for a moment that Stafford is going to sacrifice everything—his career, his creature comforts—for a woman like this? Stafford's idea of life is not love in a cottage, on a diet of bread and cheese." Elaine's voice dripped contempt.

Philippa, acutely embarrassed, avoided looking at her. She said quietly, "Elaine, has it occurred to you that Stafford may not survive—that these people may not release him alive?"

Elaine stared at her. Philippa's question had pierced the cloud of rancor in which she was enveloped. She turned away without answering.

Philippa said compassionately, "The first thing to do is to get him back alive. Does this woman offer any suggestion that might help? Does she have a purpose in coming forward except to create a sensation?"

"All I know about her is what Tom Reidy has told me. He believes that she is someone who knew Stafford in Paris, that she saw him in the company of some of these radicals there, and that she thinks she can make money out of her association with him. Of course this is all very difficult for Tom. He cannot allow any sort of public disclosure about what Stafford's mission in Paris was. It would be disastrous for the security of the United States. He is naturally more concerned about that than about any effect this might have on Stafford's private life—though, of course, he is very sympathetic to me."

"Have you told him about the letters?"

"Oh, no, no! You are the only person I have told—that I would think of telling. That is why I sent for you, Philippa. You must help me. There is no one else I can confide in."

"Yes, of course, Elaine. I shall give you all the support I can. But I don't see what I can do in a practical way."

Elaine gazed at her thoughtfully for a moment. "There is something very definite that I want you to do for me. I want you to go and see this woman and convince her that there isn't the slightest chance that she will succeed in what she is trying to do to me and Stafford."

Philippa's amazement was plain on her face. When she could speak, she said, "Elaine, you cannot seriously think that I can help you in that."

"Of course you can. I cannot approach her personally. I will not. But you can speak for me. Aside from Mamma, you are my closest relative. You must do what I ask, Philippa."

"Elaine, you overlook some very important things. Of course

we are closely related. Of course I shall give you all the support I can. But I know really nothing about Stafford. I have no idea what his relations with this woman are. You don't, either, from what you have told me. How do you know that he was not simply biding his time, when he went off to his new assignment, that he was preparing to tell you that he wanted a divorce?"

Elaine's tone was scathing. "Do you suppose for a moment, Philippa, that I could live here in this apartment with Stafford for three weeks and not know that he had any such idea in his mind? I know you've never been married, Philippa, and therefore I must allow for the fact that you haven't experienced the sort of things that married people realize. But I assure you that Stafford could not have hidden his true feelings from me like that. No. He has no intention of doing anything of that kind. Besides, you don't have to know anything about Stafford. You know a great deal about me and it is my side you are on here."

A feeling of baffled helplessness took possession of Philippa. It was a familiar sensation to her when confronted by Elaine in this mood. She said weakly, "Elaine, how would I go about this? Where is this woman? Does anyone know? How could I persuade her to talk to me?"

Elaine made an impatient gesture. "Never mind. I shall find out. Tom Reidy thinks she will try to get in touch with him. If she does not, he is going to have her placed under surveillance in any case. I can find out from him where she can be reached. But remember, Philippa, not even Tom must know what it is you are doing for me. I cannot bear the thought of anyone knowing about those letters."

Philippa, with the feeling that she was about to be thrust into unknown territory where the ground was treacherous, said as firmly as she could, "I cannot do this, Elaine, I'm sorry, but I cannot."

But Elaine paid no attention to what she said and went on talking about what she must do, how she must act. Philippa, overwhelmed by the flood of Elaine's emotion, fell silent. After some time Elaine broke off abruptly and said,

"So you see what the situation is. Now I must call downstairs and check to see if anyone from Stafford's office has been trying to reach me."

They returned to the livingroom and Elaine's attention was once more absorbed by the telephone and the doorbell.

She only cast remarks to Philippa between interruptions by the telephone and the sound of the doorbell. To Philippa, seated in a far corner of the big room, Elaine's apartment seemed like a concourse, in which there was a constant ebb and flow of people, phone calls, messengers. If I were Elaine, she thought, I'd have gone out of my mind before this, and she remembered longingly the orderly quiet of her own small apartment in Deerfield, her tranquil study into which the world rarely penetrated.

Elaine was only stimulated by the confusion, eager for each new development. Of course she is anxious about Stafford, Philippa told herself. Naturally she is on the stretch for news of him. But there was no further news. The local government, under urging by the United States, was making arrangements for the release of the political prisoners and their transportation into exile out of the country. There were newsreels showing some of them being escorted to waiting airplanes at the airport in Ciudad Nueva. But Stafford's kidnappers remained hidden behind a wall of silence.

It was late that evening, when Philippa had already withdrawn to the comparative quiet of her bedroom, that Elaine came to find her. She said excitedly, "Philippa, Tom Reidy has just called me. He says he has had a call from this woman. She told him that she is coming to Washington tomorrow to see him. If he refuses, she is threatening to make a public statement to the news media. But the important thing, Philippa, is that she told him where she is going to stay. A friend has lent her an apartment. She told him the address and the approximate time of her arrival. So now we know where you will be able to find her."

Philippa, gathering all her determination, said, "'Elaine, I've told you that I cannot do this."

But Elaine still ignored her refusal. "You must go and see her, Philippa. I'm sure she must have letters from Stafford in her possession. I am willing to buy them. But she must undertake not to bring all this out in public. Nor her affair with Stafford. What she has to say about these radicals she associated with is not my concern. Tom Reidy will have to deal with that. But she must not reveal what happened between her and Stafford in Paris."

Philippa looked at her incredulous. "Elaine, can you suppose for a moment that I would have any success in this at all? If it is sensation that she is after, of course, she is not going to be bought off. I imagine she believes she can make more money by writing accounts of her private life for the newspapers."

"Don't be so negative, Philippa. You must try."

Philippa tried another tack. "She may want a very large sum of money."

Elaine seemed to consider this for a moment. "You can at least begin negotiations with her."

They were interrupted by the phone ringing once more and Elaine did not return to talk to her before Philippa had gone to bed and put out the light.

In the morning she was awakened by Elaine's knock on her door. Elaine was in the room even before she finished saying, "Come in."

Elaine held the newspaper out to her. "Look at this."

Philippa sat up in bed and took the paper. The headlines said, "Mystery woman identified." There was a large photograph on the front page, obviously a posed studio picture. Kay's face looked up at her—Kay with her hair drawn back in an upswept hairdo, wearing large thin gold hoop earrings, gazing out with the little quirk of a smile that she had so often seen on the voyage across the Atlantic. The mystery woman, the text of the news story said, was Katherine Stephens, whose fame in the world of motion picture production was already well-established.

Elaine was saying, "It was on the early news broadcast this morning, but you were asleep. I might have known it would be someone like that. Philippa, you must go and see her this morning and tell her that it will be a great deal more to her advantage not to make a lot of public declarations."

She was about to go on when the phone rang again and she ran from the room to answer it. Philippa sat and stared at Kay's photograph. No scheme of action, no train of argument occupied her. Her mind seemed numb. Kay. Of course, Stafford was the man Kay had spoken of so vehemently. Kay was in love with Stafford. As her sense of feeling returned, she thought indignantly, could there be a greater disaster? Kay, vulnerable, foolish Kay.

Philippa got up slowly and went to take a shower. No clearer thought came to her than before. Her nerves, as if awakening slowly from a profound physical shock, began to tingle. It was as if, she told herself, Kay was present there in the bedroom. A hundred small recollections of the voyage home came to her, their meaning now obvious. But her mind seemed to refuse to accept the idea of Kay in love with Stafford. How could she have chosen someone like Stafford, absolutely condemn herself to be the victim of her own eager, uncalculating heart?

When Philippa came out of the bathroom Elaine was again in the bedroom. She announced abruptly, "That was Tom Reidy. He has given me the address of the apartment where this Stephens woman is going to stay. She is not using her own name. She is to be known there as K. Smith. I suppose even she needs some protection from the news media."

There was an unpleasant smile on Elaine's face as she made the last comment. At Philippa's silence, she went on, "Tom says that she insists that she will have an interview with the press, since he refuses to deal with her directly. He says it is far too dangerous for him to talk to her in person. Someone like that is ready to make use of an official interview to distort what has been said in it. I did not tell him, of course, that you are going to see her for me."

Elaine paused and looked at Philippa expectantly. "You are going to, aren't you? In spite of what you said last night?"

Philippa, fastening the skirt of her suit, said simply, "Yes, I will go and see her."

Elaine's face instantly regained its normal complacency. "Of course. I knew you would." She moved around to Philippa's back to fasten the zipper of her blouse. "Now, you must let me brief you on what I want you to say to her."

Philippa thought wrily, Elaine has learned the official jargon. But she said nothing aloud.

Elaine said, "When you've finished dressing, will you come to my room? I have the letters locked in my desk."

Alarmed, Philippa exclaimed, "You're not going to give them to me now?"

"Oh, no, of course not. But I want to talk to you further about them."

When she reached Elaine's bedroom Elaine was sitting at her desk in the corner, writing something on a slip of paper. She glanced up as Philippa came into the room and held the slip out to her. "Here it is. The address."

Philippa took it from her. "Have you thought, Elaine, that Reidy may object to my going there for you without his knowledge?"

Elaine smiled complacently. "What he doesn't know won't hurt him. Besides, why should he learn about it?"

"I believe you told me that he was going to have Kay—this woman placed under surveillance. That would mean that anyone

going to see her would be observed and reported to him, wouldn't
it?"

"Well, yes, I suppose so." Elaine was disconcerted for only a
moment. "But, after all, it is you who will be observed visiting her,
not me."

"Yes, but don't you think it will be a little strange? I am your
cousin. He knows you sent for me. At least I think he does. Won't
it seem strange that I should be visiting her?"

Elaine frowned thoughtfully for a moment. "Oh, well, if Tom
speaks to me about it, I shall tell him that you are a friend of hers,
that you made her acquaintance abroad."

Philippa, shocked, cried, "Elaine, that is not likely to disarm his
interest. Anyone claiming to have known her abroad would be
subject to questioning, don't you think?"

Elaine said, suddenly impatient, "Oh, Philippa, what does it
matter? You don't know anything about her, really, so of course
you're safe. All we need to do is allow time for you to see her and
persuade her to keep her mouth shut about Stafford. After that it
doesn't matter, does it? You're in no danger. How could you be, if
you know nothing?"

Philippa studied Elaine's face silently. How like you, Elaine, she
thought. You've no concern really for anyone but yourself. Aloud,
she said simply, "That is quite true. If I know nothing. But I do
know about the letters. I'm not a good liar, Elaine."

Elaine's impatience burst out. "Philippa, you must not tell
anyone why you've gone to see her, if you're questioned. You're
simply a friend of hers. You have seen the news item about her.
Naturally you want to talk to her."

"Yes, naturally I do." Something in her quiet voice caught
Elaine's ear. Elaine looked at her for a long moment, but neither
of them said anything more.

The taxi got Philippa to the address she had given the driver
about ten o'clock. It was a new building just off Washington
Circle, the sort of place offering efficiencies and one bedroom
apartments to young couples and single people who worked for
the government and other public institutions. When she asked at
the reception desk for Miss K. Smith, the clerk looked at her
suspiciously before saying, "One moment, please," and disappear-
ing into the office behind the desk. A few minutes later she came
back and said in a cautious voice, "What is you name, please? Miss
Smith said she did not want visitors or phone calls. But I can tell

her you are here."

"Tell her, please, that I am Philippa Weir. I should like to see her."

She heard the woman repeat her name twice over the telephone before turning back to say, "Miss Smith says will you come up? The number is 503. The elevator is over there."

When she stepped out of the automatic elevator and looked down the long corridor she saw Kay standing in front of an open door. She began walking towards her.

Kay, waiting apprehensively in the empty, silent hallway, saw her get off the elevator. Yes. It is Pippa. Nobody else walks just that way—that elegant, high-arched way of stepping.

Philippa, walking up to her, said simply, "Kay."

Kay's laugh was nervous. "Of course it is you, Pippa!"

"What is the matter? Were you expecting someone else?"

"No. I wasn't expecting anyone."

"You looked frightened."

"Well, I was scared for a moment. I got the idea that somebody might be using your name to get up here to see me."

"My name? There is no one really, is there, who knows we are friends?"

"That is so. It was just a wild idea." She is looking at me, thought Kay, with that reserved, cool, holding-in-the-balance expression. But I'm glad to see her. Yes, I'm very glad to see her. It is as if I was waiting for her to show up. As if I was thirsty and didn't know it and she's offered me a drink—a drink of cool, crystal pure water. That's crazy, too. I didn't think I'd ever see her again. There's that little restrained impatient gesture of hers. Of course, why are we standing out here in the hall. Kay said aloud, "Come in, Pippa, come in. I've only just got here."

That is the shortest mini-skirt I've seen her wear, thought Philippa. She has just got here and already it looks like her place. Philippa glanced around the one room apartment at the garments flung over the chairs, the sleeper sofa littered with papers, the bathroom door standing open, exhaling the warm scent of the soap Kay preferred. A tumbler half-full of whiskey and ice was set down amid the disorder of the coffee table.

Kay thought, what are you looking around like that for? Did you expect to find somebody else in here with me? She said aloud, "I'm alone."

Philippa's annoyance showed fleetingly on her face. "I hadn't supposed otherwise."

"Well, you know, you always make me feel I have to clear myself with you. You did that all the way across the Atlantic."

"That's pretty damning."

"It would be—if it was anybody but you. I don't seem to mind since it's you."

"I'm glad of that. No, I'm not really looking for something to disparage. But I wouldn't want to be—inconvenient."

Kay laughed lightheartedly. "Good old Pippa. But how did you know I was here? And what are you doing in Washington? I thought you were at Deerfield. That's hundreds of miles away."

"I'm not incarcerated there. I come to Washington sometimes. You live in New York, don't you?"

"Off and on. But how did you know where to find me?"

Philippa hesitated. "It would have been difficult to avoid seeing your picture in the paper this morning."

"My picture—Yes, of course."

She is backing off from me now, thought Philippa. She is beginning to suspect something. Aloud Philippa said, "I could not mistake it, of course."

Kay's suspiciousness had grown and hardened. "Yes, but how did you know I was here, in this apartment? You did not ask for me as Stephens downstairs, did you?"

"No. I asked for you as K. Smith."

For a few moments they fought each other with their eyes, Philippa's somber, Kay's wide and angry. "You're here because of Stafford. What connection do you have with this? Are you an agent for the government?"

Philippa, astonished, laughed. "An agent for the government? That thought never occurred to me."

But Kay was not disarmed. Angrily she demanded, "Are you connected with the State Department? Have they sent you here to spy on me? What have you come here for?"

Philippa said soberly, "If I said, for your own good, you would not believe me."

"No, I would not."

"And yet, why not, Kay? I am your friend."

Kay's laugh was sarcastic. "There's only your word for it. Say what you're here for or get out!" I'll shake it out of her, thought Kay, taking an unconsidered step closer to Philippa.

Philippa stood firm. "I'll tell you presently. But first you tell me. Is Stafford Price the man you were talking about on the ship? The man you said you were in love with?"

"That is none of your business."

"No, I suppose it isn't. None of this is my business. But that is why I have come here—because I thought he must be the man over whom you were making yourself miserable."

"That's got nothing to do with you."

Philippa sighed and turned away from their confrontation. She said wearily, "I've no intention of going away until we can talk about this."

"I don't intend to talk until I know what you're here for."

Philippa put her handbag down on the coffee table and sat down on the chair that stood beside it. "No, I'm not a spy. And yes, somebody did try to send me here to—negotiate with you. But that is not why I have come. In fact, I refused to come for that purpose."

Puzzled, Kay relaxed in spite of herself. "Negotiate with me? About what?"

Philippa said nothing and sat gazing thoughtfully at the floor. Kay, still watching her, reached for the tumbler of whiskey and stopped. She asked, "Will you have a drink?"

Philippa raised her eyes and said drily, "It is a little early in the day for me." She watched as Kay's nervous fingers closed around the glass and raised it to her lips. She is twice as jittery as she was on the ship and that was bad enough, she thought.

Kay frowned at her. Philippa could see in her eyes anger, suspicion and fear. Yes, fear. The same sort of fear she had glimpsed in Kay's eyes in their intimate moments together on the ship. The fear of someone hiding behind a facade of sophistication and bravado, someone who doubted that she could protect herself from the pain inflicted by someone else.

Philippa said, "Kay, before we go any further, I will tell you this. Stafford Price's wife is my first cousin—my only living relative."

She saw first amazement and then fury in Kay's eyes. When she could speak Kay cried, "So you're here to speak for her! She sent you here! You goddamned underhanded bitch! Get out! Get out!"

Philippa did not move. "I'm not going until we've had a chance to talk. Yes, Elaine tried to send me here to talk to you on her behalf. But I've not come here for that purpose. I've not come here on her account. I told her I would not. I'm here to talk to you about yourself."

She knew that Kay scarcely heard her or understood what she said. But after a few moments Kay said, still breathless with rage, "That's kind of you. And what do you propose to say?"

Philippa shook her head sadly. "Kay, don't be so angry with me. I'm not your enemy."

"So you're my friend." Kay's voice was filled with sarcasm. "On the basis of sharing a stateroom with me—against your choice—for five days."

"Yes, on the basis of those five days."

Kay's belligerance suddenly dropped away. She said with a gasp, "Oh, God! What are you beating about the bush for? What have you come here to say? What does she want you to say?"

"She wants me to tell you that she is ready to make it worth your while to keep quiet about Stafford. She will never agree to a divorce and she is certain that he has no intention of divorcing. He would lose too much."

Kay's voice rose hysterically. "Oh, she is going to buy me off? Is that it? She thinks everything can be bought with money—including her husband's love. Well, it can't. She does not love him. And I do. And he loves me. He is fed up with the farce of their marriage. God damn it! Don't sit there and look at me like that!" Kay's voice broke and she was half-sobbing as she turned away to hide her face.

In distress Philippa got up and walked over to her and put her hands on Kay's arms. Kay reacted violently to her touch, flinging off her hands.

"Don't touch me! Get away from me! I can't stand you!"

Philippa stepped back. "I don't know what really is between you and Stafford. But I want to tell you that I think Elaine is right when she says that he will not leave her, that he has no intention of seeking a divorce and never has had. Kay, he may have told you that, he may even have believed he might do that while he was saying it. But he doesn't now and he did not by the time he reached home from Paris."

"She has told you that! You don't know anything about it! She can make you believe anything she wants!"

"Kay, I know Stafford very slightly. But I think she is right. She is not a woman who is easily deceived."

"Well, she is deceived about this. Oh, yes, he told me we would have to wait, that he could not do anything until he had taken up his new assignment. He will act when he comes back into circulation. She had better be prepared for that."

Philippa gazed at her in silence for a moment and then said, "Kay, there is no assurance that he will come back alive. He may not even be alive now. If he does not come back, Elaine will have the last word."

A little shudder went through Kay. But she said defiantly, "She will not have the last word. I'll see to that. You can go back and tell her so."

Philippa walked back to the coffee table and picked up her handbag. "Kay, please think some more about this before you do anything. You are bound to hurt yourself. You are up against a very determined woman, surrounded by people whose interest is to support her. Can't you wait—can't you give Stafford a chance to come back and speak for himself? His statement would be far more convincing than anything you might say in speaking for him."

Kay broke out, "Elaine's words won't be any more convincing. Why don't you go and give her the same advice?"

"I will."

"She won't accept it any more than I do."

"I don't suppose she will."

"And when you go back you can tell her that I don't have any use for go-betweens."

Philippa flushed. "I have told you that I am not a go-between. I came to see you because—because I remembered our talks on the ship and I felt I'd like to save you some unhappiness, if I could."

You can take your sympathy and eat it, thought Kay. But her angry rejection faded quickly and she thought, God, I can't hate you. I can't despise you. You look like a Greek statue, cold as marble, purer than the lily because you can't be tempted. But you're not heartless. You really did come here because you remembered me and you remembered how I talked to you on the ship, how I gave myself away to you. Don't go on looking at me that way. Stop it. Go away.

Aloud Kay said, "You can find out all you want to know by watching TV."

Philippa's alarm showed on her face. "What is it you are going to do?"

Kay's smile was a grimace of anger. "I'm going to talk to the news media. I'm going to be interviewed on the noon TV broadcast. Watch it and tell your cousin to watch it."

She turned her back and paid no more attention as Philippa left the apartment and closed the door behind herself.

Elaine was talking on the telephone when Philippa got back, obviously speaking to Tom Reidy. When she hung up she said eagerly, "What did she say? Will she keep quiet?"

Philippa did not answer at once. She suddenly found it difficult to speak of Kay to Elaine.

"Well, what is it, Philippa?" Elaine demanded impatiently. "Did you have any success at all?"

"She refuses to do anything. She is going to be interviewed today on the noon news broadcast."

"Tom said he had heard that she was going to. He says they can't prevent her. But did you tell her I am going to deny everything she says, that I'll show her up for a fraud and a blackmailer?"

"Not exactly that, Elaine—"

"And did you tell her I have her letters?"

"No."

Elaine exclaimed in exasperation. "What did you tell her? Surely you made it plain that I will not put up with any threats she may make."

Philippa said slowly, "She is not open to persuasion. I tried to persuade her that she should wait until Stafford was released and was able to speak for himself. I pointed out that anything he said would be far more convincing."

Elaine's stare was full of contempt. "Convincing of what? Philippa, you cannot seriously believe that he will support what this woman says—that he will admit publicly that he had an affair with her in Paris?"

"She is certain that he loves her—that he meant what he said about the divorce." Philippa paused and held up her hand to stop Elaine from interrupting. "Elaine, if you are so certain that Stafford is not now interested in her, that he will repudiate what he told her—or what she says he told her—don't you think it would be better for you to wait, too? Let him speak for himself."

"And in the meantime I'm to sit still and let her make all these outrageous statements about him, about me—you must be out of your mind, Philippa. I cannot stand the thought."

"Of course it would be trying. But I believe it would be better for Stafford, in the end."

"And let everyone believe what she says is true? That I haven't anything to say about it? That is impossible," Elaine declared obstinately. Another thought seemed to rise in her mind. "And, besides, do you suppose for a moment that Stafford would expect me to take something like this lying down? He would not. He would expect me to defend both of us."

Would he? wondered Philippa. Well, perhaps she is right. Stafford would expect her to fight his battles. She has always done so.

Elaine had gone on speaking. "I am disappointed in you, Philippa. I thought you could at least have talked her into keeping quiet for a while."

"I don't think I'm the right person to help you in this, Elaine. I've already told you that."

"Well, I certainly can't approach the woman myself! And there is no one else I could tell all this to. You must see that. It would be extremely embarrassing to me to let anybody else know about this."

Well, the world generally is going to know about it very shortly, thought Philippa. Aloud she said, "I think you have not dealt with her the right way, Elaine."

"What other way is there? How else do you deal with someone who is threatening you like this?"

"I don't know. But I am certain that she is not the sort of woman you and Tom Reidy assume."

"Her actions speak for themselves. Why should you suppose she isn't what I think she is? Really, you are very naive, Philippa."

Philippa, harassed, said, "I know she is not what you think because I have met her before. Elaine, she shared my stateroom on the way home."

Elaine stared at her in speechless consternation. Her face became white and set, splotched with patches of red. Finally she was able to say, "Do you mean to tell me that you recognized her and said nothing to me about it? Philippa, you're extremely disloyal. How could you do such a thing?" Her anger was tinged now with tearful self-pity.

Philippa, dismayed, said hastily, "I did not tell you because I thought that perhaps she would listen to me for her own sake and that we would not have to have any further discussion of the matter. I did not go to see her as your emissary, Elaine. I had already told you that I could not be that. I have not succeeded in what I did try to do."

But she saw that Elaine was scarcely listening to her. Elaine dabbed at her eyes with her handkerchief. "Philippa, you are downright cruel! This is monstrous! I would never have believed such a thing of you."

"Why, Elaine? Because I tried to help you in my own way, not as you insisted? Very well. I am cruel, then, and heartless. But let me say that I think you are foolish to take this line of action. I think you should wait until Stafford returns and find out directly from him what he really intends to do. Does it matter what people will think? There will be a scandal in any case. If you are right in believing that Stafford has no intention of breaking with you, then he must have made promises to this girl which he had no intention of keeping. In that case, you should feel sorry for her, not angry. She is the victim, then."

Elaine's tone was scathing. "You're very eloquent in her defense, aren't you, Philippa? She must have made quite an impression on you. You're really too ingenuous for words."

Philippa, goaded into it, said sharply, "May I point out to you, Elaine, that Stafford may not come back alive? That he may be dead now. If he means anything to you, you should not be so absorbed in the idea of revenge. Revenge will not compensate you for what you have lost."

Elaine answered her angrily, but Philippa, remembering the battles of their childhood, saw that her words had had an effect, for Elaine shortly broke off their conversation.

Exhausted, Philippa sought her own bedroom and tried to calm the tumult in her own nerves that the morning had created. But within half an hour Elaine came and reminded her, excitedly, that the noon broadcast on TV would start within a few minutes. When she had gone away again Philippa thought desperately, I can't watch it. I can't stand seeing Kay expose herself like that in public. Vivid flashes came to her of Kay's face when they had talked in the stateroom about Stafford—yes, it must have been Stafford she was talking about. No, thought Philippa, I can't stay here and look at her and listen to Elaine's vindictive remarks.

She got up abruptly from her chair and opened the door of the bedroom. Elaine, she supposed, was already at the TV set, which was placed in a far corner of the livingroom. Quietly she closed the door behind her and stepped quickly across the big room. As she did so she heard Elaine's voice coming from the small recess where the phone stood. She was talking to Tom Reidy, absorbed in discussing the use that might be made of the statements Kay would make. Philippa let herself out of the front door of the apartment. As it closed behind her she thought, I forgot my handbag. But so strong was her impulse to get away from the apartment that she did not pause. She said Hello to the guard who sat in the corridor and hurried on to the elevators.

Outside on the sidewalk she stood for a moment and looked around. For November it was a warm day and she felt no need for a coat on top of her wool suit. It was sunny and still and she began to walk down the street under the tall oak trees. There was no one in sight except a nursemaid with a small child in a stroller, who sat on the low stone wall that bounded the apartment parking lot. Her need for peace and quiet made her aware of and thankful for the serene emptiness of the autumn scene. Away from Elaine's apartment she felt as if she had escaped from some concourse filled with clamor. At the far corner of the long street she stopped for a moment and then walked on down the hill that led eventually to Rock Creek Park.

She walked a long way before eventually turning back. Her thoughts had been full of Kay, she realized. Back in Deerfield her remembrance of Kay had taken on an abstract quality, as if the Kay she remembered were to some degree disembodied, had become more of an ideal companion than the flesh and blood girl who had shared her stateroom. Their encounter that morning had corrected this. Kay's bodily presence had brought back the reality of the days at sea. And how much more vivid, how much more vital that reality was!

By the time she got back to Elaine's apartment she had been gone more than an hour. She found Elaine annoyed—lunch had been held up for half an hour while they awaited her. But Elaine's reproaches were fleeting. There was obviously something else much more on her mind.

"Where did you disappear to, Philippa? I had no idea you had gone out. You missed the broadcast, of course. I came to remind you of it, you remember. It was a most outrageous performance. She made all sorts of assertions. She said she met Stafford in Paris when she was over there for a few days away from her job in London. She was working on a film, it seems. I don't know really what she has to do with films but it seems she has some sort of professional reputation. Anyway, she says she met Stafford and

that they fell in love. He is the love of her life! Imagine that! And
he was quite carried away with her! Really, you should have seen
this, Philippa. The woman should have been an actress, I should
say. And then she made a lot of other statements about Stafford.
She knew he was seeing a lot of people who were obviously
political exiles from some country in Latin America. She did not
know whether he realized who they were or not. He never
discussed this with her. Of course not! That's the only thing she
said I believe. Of course he wouldn't talk about his work to her!
Tom Reidy says that he listened to the broadcast very carefully, of
course. They may see if they can hold her for official questioning
on some grounds or other, to see if she can supply any
information about these people who abducted Stafford."

Philippa made no response to the flood of Elaine's words. After
the long thought-filled silence of her walk Elaine's vehemence
seemed remote and meaningless. She was thankful that Elaine's
preoccupation was such that she paid little attention to her
taciturnity. Throughout the afternoon the apartment was filled
with visitors and the sound of the phone ringing. Elaine herself
was swept up in the activity generated by the reports, the
speculations, the conjectures about every detail of her husband's
abduction.

There was no further news about Stafford himself. Elaine had
explained that a blanket of secrecy had been imposed by the
government of the country where he was being held. This was to
prevent anything being said or done that might jeopardize the
negotiations for his release.

In the evening Elaine insisted on turning the TV on for a re-run
of Kay's interview. Philippa, unable to escape this time,
reluctantly watched as Kay appeared on the screen, saw the
too-quick smile, the too-eager speech, the too-hasty gestures, as
Kay responded to the reporters' questions, accepted a light for her
cigarette, flared into brief anger when one interviewer insinuated
that perhaps she could not speak for Price, that he might deny
some of the statements made about him when he returned.

Elaine suddenly leaped up from her chair and turned off the set.
"Oh, I can't stand to watch that woman again! Does she really
look like that, Philippa, or is it all make-up?"

Philippa said in a neutral voice, "She is a very good-looking
girl," and went on thinking, under the barrage of Elaine's
complaints, Kay is trying hard to convince herself that she does

not doubt Stafford, that he loves her, that he is coming back to confront Elaine and straighten out their affairs. But she is not really sure of herself.

As Elaine was called away for yet another phone call, Philippa felt an almost overpowering urge to leave the apartment again, this time to go and find Kay. But what would I say to her? I have already told her what I think and she rejects what I say. Philippa struggled with this impulse the rest of the evening and into the sleepless night. It was a yearning, really, to be with Kay, she finally recognized, to give Kay whatever support she could. Perhaps the idea that she could do that was fanciful. The gap between their viewpoints seemed suddenly so great. But she remembered that, on the ship, whenever they had fallen into intimate conversation, the outward disparity in their natures seemed to dissolve and their apparent antagonism vanish. Kay, whenever they had been together for a while, had grown quieter, less restless, better tempered, yes, happier. Certainly, thought Philippa, I can be of more use to Kay than to Elaine. Elaine merely wants a presence, somebody around to appeal to, if she feels depressed, or ignore, if her attention is otherwise engaged.

She was aroused the next morning by Elaine's knock on her door. Elaine said at once as she came into the room, "Stafford has been released! He's all right but he has picked up some intestinal disease." She handed Philippa the morning paper. "Late last night, after you had gone to bed, Tom Reidy called me to tell me that the news would be out this morning. Read this while I go and make some coffee."

Philippa sat up in bed and read eagerly. During the preceding night Stafford had been taken from the remote place where he was being held. His captors had left him in an Indian's hut on the side of the mountain. He was unharmed but was suffering from a severe case of dysentery. When he was found he was taken at once to a military hospital in the nearest provincial town. He would shortly be flown to Washington and hospitalized there.

When Philippa hurried to the kitchen she found Elaine ready to talk without stop.

"You see, Philippa, I was right to be optimistic. It was just unbelievable that Stafford would not come back safely. And now we can make short work of this Stephens woman."

Philippa saw the exultant look in her eyes. "You will have to wait till Stafford recovers."

"Oh, no! There is something I intend to do at once. And you must help me, Philippa."

Philippa, alarmed, said, "What are you talking about?"

Elaine smiled triumphantly. "The letters, of course. I propose to have that cleared up before Stafford gets out of the hospital."

Philippa said earnestly, "Elaine, don't you think you ought to wait until you can at least talk to Stafford?"

Elaine's smile grew more fixed. "I do not. Philippa, you are going to see this woman and tell her that I have her letters and that I propose to confront Stafford with them. Stafford will be here at Walter Reed Hospital tomorrow. I will have this out with him as soon as I can see him. I'm sure he will see how silly it was for him to give in to her."

"But what if he says what she says is true?"

Elaine's face flushed a dark red. "Philippa, do you think for a moment that Stafford is going to sacrifice his real life and work for an ephemeral affair—especially when he knows that I am ready to forgive him and overlook the whole business?"

"And what if Kay does not give up?"

Elaine laughed angrily. "She will look a fool, won't she, if he says it is all her overheated imagination? No, Philippa, you must see her and let her know she will get nowhere by trying to pursue him. And if she resorts to blackmail, you can let her know that I shall make her letters public, so that it will be plain to everyone how she was chasing him."

Dear God! thought Philippa. Aloud she said, "What if she has letters of his to her? That would be very compromising for him and for you."

Elaine took this in for a while. "You can find out if she has any of his letters. If so, I offer to buy them."

Philippa said slowly, "Elaine, I refuse to go and see her on your behalf. You must find someone else to be your messenger. If I see Kay again, it will be as her friend as well as yours."

Elaine lashed out hotly, "You're not my friend if you are hers."

They lapsed into silence. For the rest of the morning Elaine refused to notice Philippa's presence. She was busier than ever, constantly on the telephone talking about the arrangements being made to bring her husband to Washington. On the noon broadcast Kay was mentioned. The reporters had asked her to comment on Stafford Price's release, on what she proposed to do now that he was being returned to Washington. She was quoted as saying that he must do his own talking but that she was certain he would bear out her statements.

These reports infuriated Elaine and afterwards she spent some time on the telephone talking to Tom Reidy. An unwilling eavesdropper on Elaine's half of the conversation, Philippa suddenly found she could stand the tension of cross purposes no longer. She decided to go out.

She found herself out on the sidewalk in front of the apartment house with only a vague idea of what she was going to do, except that she wanted to reach Kay. As she stood there uncertainly she realized that she might be identified as someone connected with Elaine by the news reporters sitting in cars parked at the curb. The sudden fright this gave her set her walking rapidly away to the corner to catch the first bus that was headed downtown.

When she arrived at Kay's apartment house she stopped at the reception desk to inquire if Kay was in. The woman at the desk eyed her suspiciously and said, "Is Miss Stephens expecting you?" When Philippa said yes, she added, "I don't think Miss Stephens is in. She does not answer her phone." She paused to look carefully at Philippa. "You were here the other day, weren't you?"

Philippa said yes again and the woman replied, "You could go up and see if she will answer her doorbell. She just doesn't want reporters."

Philippa walked hurriedly to the elevator and pushed the button for the fifth floor. When she reached Kay's door and rang the bell she could hear the door chimes but for a while there was no other sound. She must be here, I must see her, she thought desperately. She pressed the button again and listened intently as the soft chimes once more died away. After what seemed a long while she heard an unidentifiable sound in the room beyond the door. Then she heard Kay's voice say impatiently, "What do you want?"

"Kay, it's Philippa."

Kay opened the door abruptly. In the dim light of the little hall, against the brightness of the windows beyond, Philippa could see at first only her silhouette. She was wearing a short-skirted dress and her hair hung to her shoulders, as it had on their first meeting on shipboard.

Kay took a step back to let Philippa come in. She said, "I don't want to hear anything more about your cousin."

Her tone was abrupt and firm but there was no rancor in it. At least she is not angry with me now, thought Philippa.

Aloud Philippa said, "I've not come to speak for her. I've just come—to see you."

"To see me? What for?"

"Because, I suppose, I want very much to try and keep you from hurting yourself more than you have."

She expected angry rejection but Kay merely turned away into the room and said mockingly, "Well, since this is a rescue operation, you might as well come and sit down."

She walked over to the sofa and dropped down on it. Philippa sat down in the armchair. Kay lit a cigarette.

Philippa said, "I heard your statements on TV. So did Elaine, of course. You know that Stafford will be in the hospital here in Washington today."

Kay's only response was a nod.

"Elaine will see him as soon as he has been officially interviewed by people from the Department. She is certain that he will tell her that he has no intention of seeking a divorce, that his affair with you in Paris was just that, an affair."

Still Kay made no remark.

"She has also convinced herself that Stafford succumbed to you because you pursued him. She knows he gives in easily to women. She says that if you don't leave him alone she will demonstrate this to the world at large."

"God! How is she going to do that?"

"While Stafford was being held as a hostage she went through his private papers. She found your letters to him. She says they amply support what she says."

Kay was very white. "You mean to say she read my letters to him?"

"It would seem so," said Philippa noncommittally.

"Of all the damnable, lowminded things to do!" Kay's voice rose to an hysterical pitch.

Philippa cut in sharply. "Would you expect her not to read them, having found them openly among his things and suspecting what they were? Of course, she would read them, Kay. That is chiefly what I've come to tell you. Believe me, you are dealing with a very obstinate woman who will not be squeamish about taking any measures to protect what she considers to be her property. Kay, I know Elaine very well. I've known her from childhood. Please listen to me."

"Hell! Why did he leave them around for her to find?"

"You will have to ask him that. Perhaps—" Philippa paused to look at Kay. Yes, she thought, I am going to say it to her. "Perhaps he wanted Elaine to find them. Perhaps he wanted to let her know what had happened in Paris, so that she would come to his defense—save him from something he no longer wanted."

Kay's anger mounted to fury. "Did she tell you to come and say that to me?"

"No."

For a while Kay silently struggled with herself. Finally she said, her voice shaking, "I ought to throw you out of here. What you are telling me is that I am a silly fool and Stafford is a spineless woman chaser. And I tell you that that is not true. He does love me. I love him as I have never loved anyone before. But what the devil do you know about loving anybody? You haven't got blood enough in your veins. Damn it! Why don't you leave me alone?"

She watched Philippa's normally pale face grow paler and her jaw set rigidly. Yes, I've got to her there, thought Kay. And I hate myself for doing it. Why? Because I think she's my friend. Yes, I do. She isn't cold to me. That's a silly idea for me to have—to think she makes an exception of me to everybody else in the world. But I know somehow that it's true. There she sits, made of marble, without the slightest expression on that beautiful cold face, and yet I feel warm and comforted when she is with me. What a silly ass I am!

Aloud she said in a calmer voice. "What else did you come to say?"

Philippa swallowed before she spoke in her normal unruffled voice. "I suggested to Elaine that you might have—that you probably do have letters from Stafford that would prove embarrassing to him and to her."

Kay stared at her. Suddenly she laughed and though there was a trace of hysteria in the sound of it, Philippa sighed in relief. Kay asked, "What did she say to that?"

"She is prepared to buy them from you."

Kay's laughter became frankly hysterical as she dropped her face into her hands and rocked back and forth. She did not resist when Philippa reached over and took hold of her shoulder.

"Quiet down, Kay. You're overwrought."

Kay said with a gasp. "What is she afraid of—that they will prove that Stafford did promise me what I say he did? That they will be proof that she's wrong and I'm right?"

Philippa did not answer at once and after a moment Kay said, "Go on and say what you're not saying."

"Perhaps it is more complicated than that. Elaine is quite ready to believe that Stafford said a lot of things to you while he was with you in Paris which he now would like forgotten. But they cannot be, can they, if he put them in writing to you?"

"Is that what you believe?"

"I have no reason to believe one thing rather than another. I do not know Stafford well. Perhaps he is really the man you say he is. It seems to me more likely that Elaine knows him better. But whatever the case, I assure you that I know Elaine very well and she has a will of iron. She will break you, Kay."

"And you think she has already broken him! Do you really think she can make him change his mind?"

Philippa said, hesitating, "I don't think she needs to do that. I don't think he needs to change his mind. He may have been quite sincere when he told you in Paris that he loved you, that he loved you well enough to make sacrifices for you. But I think he probably had already changed his mind by the time he got back to Washington and Elaine. No! No! Don't fly out at me like that, Kay. I can't bear to have you curse at me like that! I must tell you what I believe the truth to be."

"Even if it kills me!" Kay was almost sobbing with rage.

For a while neither of them spoke. Then, having conquered her feelings, Kay said scornfully, mimicking Philippa's manner of speaking, "So for the sake of everybody's peace of mind I am to return his letters. One must always avoid the difficult, the embarrassing. Nothing is ever important enough to make a scandal about." She broke off and changed back to her own voice. "Damn it! We don't all keep our feelings on ice all the time!"

"Kay, it doesn't help for you to mock me."

"Oh, forget it! But you give me enough provocation. When you were here the other day, you pointed out that neither his wife nor I should be trying to speak for Stafford, that when he got back he might not support either of us. Well, Elaine hasn't seen him, hasn't talked to him yet. I'm willing to wait to see what he will say when he is able to talk."

Philippa looked at her in silence. She has had very little sleep, she thought. She is really haggard. A pang went through Philippa. Why must she be so engrossed in him? She will have nothing but grief from this situation. I cannot believe that Stafford would make himself unhappy about her as she makes herself over him. He will be ready to shelter behind Elaine.

Kay suddenly asked, "Do you suppose there is any chance that they'd let me see Stafford?"

"See him? Not now, I don't suppose. Even Elaine won't be able to see him until he has been interviewed by the government officials. There is a lot being made of security in his case, you know. Kay, do you realize that you are under some suspicion youself, for associating with these radicals in Paris?"

"Oh, that nonsense!" Kay exclaimed contemptuously. "Of course I had nothing to do with them except as people who were with people I knew. I used to wonder why Stafford paid so much attention to them."

"Perhaps it would be as well not to call yourself to the attention of Stafford's colleagues."

"Or I may be railroaded to Siberia? Don't worry about me, Pippa. I haven't a clue as to what Stafford was doing in Paris. He really kept his lip buttoned on that. So you think they won't let me see him?"

"I don't know."

"You don't think I'd be officially kidnapped, do you, if I turned up at the gate at Walter Reed and said I'd come to see him?"

Philippa, glad to see the light of mischief in Kay's eyes, said quickly, "There's no telling."

"Oh, Pippa, you're a tonic! You do try hard to cheer me up, don't you?" More relaxed, she ruminated for a moment before she said, "Poor Stafford. He doesn't know what he is coming back to, does he?"

Philippa, instantly annoyed, retorted, "He must be quite familiar with Elaine's tactics by now."

Kay studied her thoughtfully. "You don't like him, do you?"

Philippa looked surprised. "Why, I don't know him well enough to know whether I like him or not. I have only Elaine to go by."

"Ah, Elaine. I'd hate to form an opinion of anybody on what Elaine said about them. Her opinion of me, for instance. Do you go by that?"

Philippa felt herself flushing. "Of course not. I came to know you for yourself before Elaine said anything to me."

"Well, I'm glad of that." Kay spoke with satirical heartiness. "What does she tell you I am doing—outside of being a harpy who wants to ruin her husband?"

"She thinks you are seeking publicity—for the sake of making money out of it."

"I get all the publicity—of the kind I want—that I need. You can tell her that."

"There is no point in my telling Elaine anything."

"So what will you say to her when you get back from here?"

"I don't know. She was not speaking to me when I left her apartment."

Kay's eyes lighted up. "Is it as bad as that?" Kay gazed at her for a moment. "You mean to say you quarreled with her about me?"

Philippa, annoyed with herself, said sharply, "Elaine and I have never been easy companions."

"Pippa, you're evading the issue again. If that's the case, why are you there with her?"

"Because she sent for me. I felt I had to come. I did not know anything about you being involved, of course."

There was almost a smile on Kay's face. "Upright, uptight Pippa. So you rallied around your one and only relative. What happened when you found out about me?"

"She wanted me to come and bargain with you about Stafford. I said I didn't think that was something I could help her with. But Elaine ignores one's refusal to do something, if her mind is set upon it. I came to see you on my own. She was angry when she found out about that."

Kay was eyeing her critically. "So that's it. Pippa, why are you taking my part in this?"

Philippa felt the tears come into her eyes. She turned away so that Kay would not see them. When she could speak naturally she said, "Perhaps this will strike you as absurd, but I feel you are much more my friend than Elaine ever was."

Kay smiled at her mischievously. "She's not your friend. She's your cousin." Kay got up from the sofa and moved restlessly about the room. "If she is not speaking to you, do you have to go back to her now?"

"I have no inclination to."

"Well, come and have dinner with me. I had no lunch and I'm hungry. There's a place down the street where we can have a good steak. Let's forget Elaine for a while."

The restaurant was not yet crowded and they were able to

choose a table in a corner away from other diners. This is like being on the ship, Philippa thought. They sat over a drink and talked companionably. As Kay became absorbed in describing her work she grew easy and relaxed. Philippa thought, dear Kay. When you are yourself, not someone else's puppet, you glow. Your face lights up. You lose that haggard, badgered look in your eyes, which are beautiful and sparkle. Why must you torment yourself over this pointless affair? He'll not give a second thought to abandoning you when Elaine confronts him.

Kay suddenly looked up at her. "What are you looking at me like that for, Pippa?"

"Was I looking at you?"

"Of course you were. It's not so dark in here that I can't see you." When Philippa did not answer, she said petulantly, "All right. Keep it to yourself. Are you brooding about those letters again?"

"I was not thinking of them," said Philippa, regretting the shattering of their peaceful communion. "But, since you mention them, what are you going to do about them?"

Kay's eyes were angry now. "You can tell Elaine that I am going to write my memoirs and of course I'll publish them in full."

"Elaine has no sense of humor. She will not know that you are joking."

"Who said I was joking?"

Philippa drew in her breath. "If Stafford means as much to you as you have told me he does, I do not believe that you would make a public show of your feelings."

Kay said savagely, "Then you do not agree with Elaine, do you? I'm not just a mercenary woman ready to sell my soul for a fat blackmail payment."

Philippa said gently, "Kay don't speak to me like that. You know very well I should never suppose anything of the sort."

Kay relented, saying wearily, "No, you've always given me the benefit of the doubt. Well, in fact, I shall not give the letters to anyone but Stafford himself."

Again the subject lapsed between them but the rest of the meal was silent and uneasy. When they left the restaurant they walked together back to the corner of the street where Kay's apartment house stood. They stood for a moment without speaking, until Philippa said, "Kay, shall we meet again?"

Kay, as if roused from deep preoccupation, gave her a strange look. "That's a funny thing to ask me. You've come to see me at your own choice. You say you haven't come from Elaine."

Philippa said quickly, "That's quite true, Kay."

A slight smile appeared on Kay's face. "Oh, I believe you! I don't think you're very good at lying. But what's the point of coming to see me, Pippa? Even if Elaine didn't send you, you're in her camp, aren't you?"

"No! I am not. I meant, shall we meet again before I go back to Deerfield?"

"Are you about to?"

"There is no reason for me to stay here now."

She was surprised when Kay suddenly seized her arm. "Pippa, don't go away without coming to see me again. I do need you, Pippa."

Philippa, rooted to the ground by the wave of longing that overcame her, could not speak. Oh, Kay, Kay! She thought. What am I to do?

Kay was shaking her arm. "Wake up, Pippa! Have you gone to sleep standing up? Well, good night."

Elaine said impatiently, angrily, as Philippa came into the apartment, "Where on earth have you been? I really cannot understand you, Philippa! This is the second time you have completely ignored the fact that I expected you to a meal."

Philippa, trained to be punctilious about such things, thought vaguely, I should have called her before I went to dinner with Kay. But she felt no real distress. I cannot tell her I have had dinner with Kay.

Aloud she said, "I did not think you would want me to disturb you, Elaine."

Elaine, recognizing the veiled reference to the fact that they had quarreled, replied, "I was really alarmed. Do you realize that it is after nine?"

"I hope you did not wait too long for me."

"Well, Tom Reidy dropped in, so we went ahead. He came to tell me that Stafford is already at Walter Reed. Perhaps I shall be able to see him tomorrow."

"I'm very glad to hear that."

"I cannot wait to settle this business of the Stephens woman. When I go to see him I shall take her letters with me."

Philippa protested. "Stafford will be exhausted, Elaine. Wouldn't it be better to wait till he has a chance to rest? He must have had quite an ordeal."

Elaine's eyes glittered at her. "Oh, no. I am going to have it out with him as soon as I have a moment alone with him. I must know how we stand immediately. You forget, Philippa, that he never told me anything about what happened in Paris. You forget that he came back from Paris and said nothing to me about what happened there. He let me believe that there was nothing to threaten our normal life together."

"Isn't that what you believe is the fact—that Stafford never had any intention of continuing his affair?"

"Certainly. But obviously I cannot let him go on thinking that I'm in the dark about it all. I really resent that, Philippa."

"Well, undoubtedly you are the best judge of your relationship with Stafford. But I should tell you at once, Elaine, that I am going back to Deerfield. You have no further need of me now, I'm sure."

Elaine exclaimed. "Oh, you cannot do that, Philippa! You told me that you had made arrangements to stay away at least a week. You don't think I've heard the last of that woman, do you? And I cannot deal with her myself."

"You must find someone else to act for you. I cannot."

Elaine said angrily. "You are right there. You certainly are not the person to act for me. It is obvious that you are completely swayed by her. I cannot understand that. If you were a man, I should say she had used her sexual attractions to seduce you."

"Then there is no reason why I should not return to Deerfield."

The decision in her voice penetrated Elaine's self-preoccupation. She changed the tone of her voice. "Philippa, I really feel quite badly that you have not given me your loyalty, as I expected you to. But I don't want you to go. I do need you here until at least I have had a chance to talk to Stafford. It will be very unkind of you to desert me now, before I can make sure where I stand."

Philippa, recognizing the nearest that Elaine could come to apology and an appeal for sympathy, said grudgingly, "All right. I shall stay until you've seen Stafford."

The next few hours Philippa spent listening as patiently as she could to the endless speculations, recriminations and half-tearful reproaches that poured from Elaine. It is just as well, she thought, that I agreed to stay. Even though she is only concerned with herself, still she is deeply unhappy and I should not withhold what comfort I can give her.

But by the time she was able to say goodnight and close her bedroom door her nerves were drawn taut. She stood for a while by the window, staring down at the patch of empty street lit by the street lamp. It was only now that she realized that it was not Elaine's laments that had told on her. In fact, she had soon ceased to listen to Elaine. It was the state of her own emotions that caused this exhaustion, this despair. For hours now, for days, she had been rejecting, not Elaine and Elaine's tenacious possession of Stafford, but Kay's yearning for the man who had captured her heart. Every fibre in her fought against Kay's obsession.

I love her, she said aloud in the half-dark room. I am jealous. I hate Stafford. I hate all the men she ever had anything to do with. I want her for myself. And how can I have her when she can think only of Stafford?

She went no further for a moment. It was simple enough to say, I love Kay. That could be an abstract idea, a bodiless emotion, a sympathy of the spirit—the sort of muted, reason-dominated liking that Kay would call bloodless. But that is not what I feel now. I love Kay totally. I long for her body. I writhe inwardly at the idea that she has gone to bed with Stafford, that she longs now to go to bed with him again. Yes, this is desire and I desire Kay.

She stopped herself to look directly at what she had at last acknowledged. For the first time in her life she knew desire, desire for a particular person, desire for Kay—naked, driving desire. But Kay wanted Stafford.

Her night was sleepless. As morning drew near she reached a state of nervous tension that prompted her to get up and once more contemplate the idea of going back to Deerfield forthwith. That was really where she belonged, out of this conflict of body and soul. She should never have left her well-ordered life. She should have summoned up that last ounce of determination to refuse Elaine's entreaties. Kay would then have remained in her memory as a disembodied love, to be treasured secretly. She wondered how she would have felt then, if, being in Deerfield, far from the scene of events, she had seen Kay's face and heard Kay's voice on TV. And at that point she knew that she would have suffered as great anguish as that she felt now.

She wished she had not promised Elaine that she would stay. It was a refinement of torture to remain where she heard nothing but the endless mention of Stafford, of Kay, of Elaine's determination to end their affair. Undoubtedly Elaine would succeed. And then, what of Kay? Perhaps she could help Kay pick up the pieces. But she shrank from the thought of being Kay's buffer, of seeing and hearing Kay's despair. If she left Washington now, simply abandoned all the promises she had made, she could at least gain for herself the peace that came from distance.

She got up and dressed. When she came out of her bedroom the apartment was silent except for the sound of the refrigerator and the electric clock in the kitchen. The livingroom was in dimly lit disarray. The glasses she and Elaine had used were still where they had been left, the cushions on the sofa and upholstered chairs were unshaken, the drapes at the windows were still drawn. Elaine must have gone to bed without thought of her usual housewifely chores.

Philippa stepped quietly to the door of Elaine's room and quietly opened it. The room was in darkness, the blinds and curtains tightly closed, and she could hear Elaine's light snore. Probably Elaine had taken sleeping pills and would not wake for some time yet. If she was going to leave and go back to Deerfield, this was her opportunity.

But even as she thought this she knew she had decided to stay. And it was not because of Elaine. She was staying because of Kay. She could not bear the thought of going away and cutting herself off from the chance of seeing Kay once more.

In the end she straightened the livingroom and settled down with the morning paper. Without real interest she read the re-hash of yesterday evening's news, the reports and speculations about the plot in which Stafford had become involved as a hostage. There was only one brief reference to Kay. A small item on an inside page said that U.S. government investigators were satisfied that the woman who had claimed to be Stafford Price's girl friend in Paris had no real connection with the group of radicals with which he had associated. Her much publicized revelations were dismissed as having no bearing on his kidnapping or the motives of his abductors. The reasons for her alleged disclosures were unexplained.

Well, at least, thought Philippa, Kay is out of that particular danger.

It was noon before Elaine emerged, nervous and irritable. Philippa braced herself for a resumption of the flow of petulant complaints that had filled the evening before. It was with relief that she discovered that Elaine was entirely taken up with the prospect of visiting Stafford in the hospital and spent most of the afternoon on the telephone talking with various people to this end. At eight o'clock in the evening she received the summons she was expecting. Hurrying out of the apartment she called back, "Wait up for me, Philippa. I may need you."

PART III

It was past midnight when Elaine returned from the hospital, animated, voluble. Her voice was confident, almost strident with self-assurance.

"He's in top shape. The antibiotics took care of the parasites he picked up. He says he feels fine. And I was right. Of course everything that woman said is nonsense. Stafford loves me. He has no intention, never had, of getting a divorce. Oh, he admits he had an affair with her. It is obvious she seduced him. I've always known he is very susceptible—especially if a good-looking woman throws herself at his head. He can't bear to disappoint anyone. It is an endearing weakness of his, really."

Philippa, feeling drained and helpless from the long vigil filled with her own hopeless problem, said nothing.

"He is very upset about all this publicity, of course. He can't tell me anything about the reasons why he was kidnapped and all that. That's top secret. But all this business about his promises to her that he was coming back to divorce me and marry her—Philippa, it is all so outrageous that even now I can't credit that she actually made such statements. She must be completely conscienceless."

When Philippa still remained silent, she went on, after a glance at her, in a different tone of voice. "You say you know her. Certainly you've met and talked to her. What kind of a creature is she? Is she really unbalanced or just mercenary?"

Stung into speech, Philippa said, "She is neither one. You've seen her on television. She is an unusually attractive young woman. I am not surprised that men find her irresistible."

"Do they?" Elaine's voice was charged with skepticism.

"Yes, they do. She has no trouble attracting men. In fact, sometimes she finds her own attractiveness a nuisance."

"Dear me." Elaine's voice was now sarcastic. "I suppose you observed evidence of this on board ship. I should have thought she would be a troublesome sort of woman for someone like you to share a stateroom with."

In spite of herself Philippa flushed. "She was not troublesome at all. She showed me every consideration."

Elaine eyes her contemptuously. "You're quite her champion,

aren't you? That's very odd, Philippa. You're usually far more reserved in your opinion of people. I would never have supposed that you would associate with that sort of woman."

Philippa lost her temper. "Elaine, you're speaking in ignorance. She is not that sort of woman."

Elaine was equally angry. "She tried to seduce my husband, didn't she? She deliberately tried to break up my marriage."

"May I point out that, even if she had any such intent, she could hardly have succeeded without Stafford's help? Is he such a foolish weakling that any woman can lead him astray?"

Elaine, her eyes overflowing with angry tears, reached for a tissue. Her voice was tearful as she said, "Philippa, I've never known you to be so cruel. I've been having a perfectly dreadful time this last week, and you haven't even tried to comfort me."

Dear God! thought Philippa. Yes, I suppose I should comfort her. I suppose I should see things from her point of view. It has been mine up till now. But I cannot listen to her speak of Kay so.

Aloud she said, going closer to Elaine and putting her hand on Elaine's shoulder, "I did not mean to hurt you. It is hard for me to pretend about my feelings. You know that, Elaine. I am truly sorry for you. I think you have been shabbily treated. But please remember that Stafford is at least equally to blame. He admits to having been unfaithful to you. And you have told me this is not the first time. The trouble is that he knows he can always get around you. He knows you will stick by him no matter how he behaves."

For a moment Elaine accepted her sympathy and put her head down on Philippa's shoulder. Philippa tried not to shrink away. They had never been used to endearments, to caresses. In their family these had never been natural means of expressing fondness or tenderness. Since her mother had died Philippa had lost entirely the habit of bestowing kisses and hugs on anyone.

To her relief, Elaine drew away almost at once, dabbing at her eyes. "At least, he always comes back to me. He will never really leave me."

Philippa looked at her with genuine pity. What a poor return for one's devotion, she thought. But she silently agreed that Elaine was right. Stafford would never risk Stafford's comfort. Stafford would always come home to mother. Aloud Philippa said, "If you're satisfied with that, Elaine, there is nothing more to be said."

Elaine, her equanimity restored, said complacently, "Philippa, you have never been married, you have never even been in love. You've never shared your life with someone. If you had, you would know that one must always make some compromises. It is a question of what is most important to one—to possess one's loved one regardless of anything else. It is fortunate that you have never felt desire for a man. You would never compromise, you would never be willing to forgive."

Philippa, irritated, said shortly, "Elaine, you need not dwell on my lack of feeling. After all, that is not what is in question here. You are concerned with Stafford. According to you, he completely repudiates Kay."

"Kay? Oh, that woman. Oh, yes, completely. He has no use for her now, especially after all this publicity—this public display of her private life."

"You are not mistaken there? You are not deceiving yourself, Elaine, because of what you wish to believe?"

Elaine flushed angrily. "Certainly not! Don't you understand, Philippa? I know Stafford very well. He is relieved that I now know what he did in Paris, since I have forgiven him. We can both wipe it all out now."

"I see."

Something in her manner caused Elaine to look at her closely and say, "There is still one thing that bothers me considerably. Those letters."

"Kay's?"

"No. I told him that I had found her letters to him. He knows that I know what she said in them. But I asked him about the letters he wrote to her. I pointed out to him that she could use them against him."

"And what did he say?"

"He says they are not very important. He doesn't think she would use them and anyway he could talk her into giving them back to him." Elaine paused, frowning. After a moment she went on, "I don't like that."

"You don't like what?"

"Well, I don't like the idea that she has letters from him in her possession. And especially I don't like the idea of his having any more to do with her. He has promised me that he will not see her again."

So you really don't trust him, thought Philippa. Oh, Kay, why did you have to choose him? Why did you have to pick someone so shallow, so shifting? My poor darling.

Philippa became aware that Elaine had gone on talking. "Really, Philippa, it would be far better, since you know her, if you would go and see her again and offer her money for those letters."

With carefully controlled calm Philippa said, "I don't think she would take money for them."

"Why not? Surely she must realize now that she has lost the advantage. I'll be generous enough. On the contrary, I believe she would be eager to give them up if I make it worth while."

Philippa, with a great effort, maintained a neutral manner. "Perhaps Stafford could persuade her to exchange them for her letters to him."

Elaine's face lighted up. "Why, that is brilliant, Philippa! But not Stafford. He is too susceptible. You can take them to her and offer to exchange, as you say, acting for me."

Philippa looked at her aghast. "Elaine, you cannot be serious."

"Of course I am serious. Philippa, you are exasperating when you get an idea fixed in your mind. You persist in thinking this woman isn't swayed by money. Of course she is. There is nothing highminded about her. You're simply being naive—putting yourself in her place. You've got that sort of romantic streak in you. No. You must act for me. You can point out that she will be much better off having her own letters back."

Valiantly Philippa clung to her self-control. "Elaine, the letters are not yours. They were written to Stafford. Won't you feel any embarrassment at admitting so openly that you have spied on his private affairs?"

Elaine bridled with indignation. "His private affairs? He is my husband. He does not—he should not—have any private affairs that are not also mine."

"That isn't the point of view of a lot of married people nowadays."

"Well, it is mine and Stafford knows that it is." Elaine got up abruptly and left the room.

She has gone to get the letters, thought Philippa and cringed at the image of herself carrying them to Kay and bargaining over them. And yet if I don't do it, Elaine will get someone else, someone who will have not the slightest regard for Kay's feelings.

Elaine came back into the room with several envelopes in her hand. "There are only four. I think Stafford must have thrown the rest away. Here. Take them, Philippa. You must go and see her."

Reluctantly Philippa took them from her. Even then she said, "Elaine, I haven't said I would go."

"You must, Philippa, you must."

After a pause Philippa said, "I am leaving for Deerfield tomorrow. There is a through flight in the morning and one in the evening. I had thought to take the morning plane."

Elaine exclaimed impatiently. "Why, look," she said, pointing to the mantel clock. "It is already four o'clock. There is no point in your trying to leave by the morning flight. If you wait till the evening one, you will have time to go and see this woman. Let's go to bed now, Philippa. I'm going to have a hectic day tomorrow, I know."

She bustled about the room, purposefully straightening the furniture and clearing away newspapers and glasses. Even after she had left the room to go to her bedroom, saying goodnight, Philippa stood with the letters in her hand, unable to resolve her own indecision. She looked down at them as if she held in her hand something dangerous, something capable of destroying her. And so they might, when she presented them to Kay. For if Kay refused to accept the motive that led her to bring them to her, if the fact that she was ostensibly Elaine's spokesman caused Kay to reject her completely, then she would be destroyed.

But they were also a passport, a passport into Kay's life. If she could only know how to use them—if Kay would only see in them the folly of her obsession with Stafford—

I will postpone going to Deerfield, Philippa said aloud to herself. I will go back on the evening flight.

In the morning, when Elaine finally awoke, she was prepared. She said, as they shared a midmorning cup of coffee in the kitchen, "I will take those letters and see what Kay has to say. But I must warn you, Elaine, that I am not going to undertake any bargaining. If she rejects your offer, that is that. I shall stop by and see her on my way to the airport this afternoon. If she makes no question of accepting your offer, I shall call you from the airport. Otherwise I shall send the letters back to you by mail. These are the only terms on which I will act for you, Elaine."

"Well, good gracious, Philippa! It is only eleven o'clock. If you went now—"

She was interrupted by the telephone. The call was obviously from Tom Reidy and Elaine was at once absorbed in a conversation that caused her to forget even that Philippa still sat in the same room with her. The talk was all of Stafford, of his probable release from the hospital in a few days' time, of his role in the continuing problem of the revolutionaries who had kidnapped him. When Elaine put down the phone she announced that she was going back to the hospital in an hour or so's time to see Stafford.

"So I shan't be here, then, when you leave, Philippa. I really do think you should postpone going back to Deerfield until you can help clear up the business about the letters."

But Philippa said stubbornly, "I am going back this evening. I shall let you know about the letters when I can. She may not even be home, in which case I shall take them along with me."

She expected Elaine to protest, but the train of thought that had been aroused in Elaine's mind by the telephone conversation still dominated and she turned away without further comment. Throughout lunch she talked only of Stafford and what his official problems would be.

Alone in the quiet apartment after Elaine had left she packed her bag and debated how much time she should allow herself. Her plane left at seven. She should, she supposed, give herself an hour to stop by Kay's apartment. She would leave at five o'clock then, to allow for delays in the rush hour traffic to the airport. But in the end her impatience got the better of her and it was only four when she went out of the door and sought a cab.

In the cab she took the letters out of her handbag and examined them. They were written on thin airmail paper and the envelopes, neatly slit open, bore French and English stamps. Kay must have written them in the short interim between Stafford's departure from Paris and her own embarkation at Southampton. Elaine had felt no compunction at taking the letters from the envelopes and reading them. Philippa thought, I'm hopelessly out of step with the times. The idea of invading someone else's privacy repelled her. But she knew there was another reason why she could not bear the thought of reading these letters, a reason she was reluctant to frame even to herself. In them Kay had undoubtedly bared her heart, bared her heart of the love she had felt for Stafford. And I want that love for myself, Philippa cried to herself. I could die for want of it.

This time when she entered the lobby of Kay's apartment house the woman at the reception desk merely waved to her in a friendly fashion as she crossed quickly to the elevators. Obviously the heat of publicity was off so far as Kay was concerned, thought Philippa. She rang Kay's bell and listened for the chimes. Nothing happened, so she tried again. On the third try she heard sounds and presently Kay's voice, hoarse and impatient, said, "Who's there?"

"Philippa. I am on my way to Deerfield."

Kay opened the door and stepped back to let her in. She was wearing a long robe of filmy material that clung to her body. It was unfastened and as she moved it gaped to show her naked body. When she followed Kay into the one room she saw that the sofa bed was still open and tumbled. The ashtrays overflowed, Kay's garments were strewn about the room. The breeze from the open window had cleared the air but there was still a scent of stale whiskey and cigarette smoke.

Kay looked pale and disheveled and her blonde hair hung about her face. She stared dully at the small suitcase that Philippa set down out of the way.

"Did I waken you, Kay?" Philippa asked gently.

Kay shook her head. Philippa, troubled by the strange look in her eyes, tried to speak casually. "I stopped by because I had told you that I'd see you again before leaving Washington." Even in her own ears her voice sounded flat, precise, cold.

The faintest smile appeared on Kay's lips. "You always keep you word, don't you, Pippa?"

"Don't make fun of me, Kay."

Kay gave her a glance of surprise. "Make fun of you? That's the last thing I want to do, Pippa. I've discovered it is not such a joke when somebody can be counted upon to keep their word."

Disconcerted, Philippa looked away from her.

"Sit down, Pippa. We don't have to keep standing here."

Kay herself dropped down on the sofa. After a silence she said, "I need some coffee. And a hair of the dog."

"Don't you have any orange juice? Or milk?"

Kay's laugh was short. "Ever the soul of right thinking, aren't you? No. I never drink milk and I haven't any orange juice. But there are some little cans of tomato juice in the refrigerator."

"Then drink one. You haven't had anything to eat today, have you?"

Again Kay studied her. "You never give up, do you?" As she got up to go to the refrigerator in the kitchen, she added, "You

wouldn't be Pippa, if you did. All right, I'll skip the whiskey."
When she came back with the glass of juice in her hand, she said,
"I've put the water on for some coffee. Have you had a fight with
Elaine?"

"Not what you'd call a fight."

"No, I guess not. From what I've heard, she is good at putting
you in the wrong without giving you the satisfaction of a real
fight."

Philippa, anxious to state her errand but uncertain how to
begin, said nothing. Kay sat silently sipping the juice. Her eyes
were fixed on the floor and she looked deeply dejected and
unmindful that she was not alone.

"Kay," Philippa said at least, hesitantly. "Elaine has seen
Stafford in the hospital and talked to him."

Without looking up Kay said, "I know."

"You know!"

Kay raised her eyes and Philippa saw that they were full of rage.
"Yes, I know! I talked to Stafford on the phone this morning."

Philippa waited for her to go on but she did not. So Philippa
said, "Elaine went to see him last night. She was with him for
some time. When she came back to the apartment she said that she
had confronted Stafford with your letters and told him that she
knew all about the affair he had had with you in Paris. She
informed me that he said he had no intention of leaving her—that
his affair with you was over. Kay, I do not know whether that is
the truth. I do not know for sure whether Elaine has interpreted
what he said as she wished or not. I do not know whether he
deliberately lied to her."

Philippa looked anxiously at Kay as she spoke, alarmed at her
failure to make any response. But Kay had once more dropped her
head and she could not see her face. She waited in suspense.

Presently Kay said in a harsh voice, "Go on and tell me the rest
of it."

Philippa, writhing inwardly in shame, said, "Elaine is unable to
believe that you really love Stafford. She thinks your motives are
mercenary. She thinks you can be bought off. She dreads scandal.
So she calls you a blackmailer who wishes to profit by her
husband's weakness."

Kay raged, "I am supposed to be doing this—I'm supposed to be
willing to make a fool of myself in public just for money. That is
what I have done—made a fool of myself. I'm not supposed to care

about exposing my private life so long as I get paid for it! I'm not
supposed to feel any shame about publicly airing my deepest
feelings! All I want is money!" Kay had raised her head again and
Philippa saw that her eyes were filled with tears of rage.

"She has no intention of giving Stafford up, Kay. She will fight
you with every means in her power. She has powerful weapons
and Stafford knows that very well."

The kettle on the stove suddenly whistled piercingly. Kay
leaped to her feet, cursing. She rushed to the kitchenette
muttering, "I don't know why anybody would want one of those
things."

"It does prevent burned-up kettles, if you're absentminded."
Philippa got up. "Here, give it to me. I'll make the coffee."

When she returned with the two cups and placed them on the
coffee table she said, "Come on. Have some, Kay. You look as if
you have been on a liquid diet. Shall I get you something to eat?"

Kay was standing with her back towards her. "I don't want any
food." Suddenly she whirled around. "What have you really come
here for? Is this some sort of trick—to pretend that you're
sympathetic to me just to get around me?"

Philippa turned pale. "Surely you know me better than that,
Kay." She realized that she was close to tears. The sleepless nights,
her hopeless longing had brought her to the verge of collapse. In
her effort to control herself she lost track of Kay. She was
surprised to feel Kay's arm go round her shoulders. Kay's voice
said, close to her ear, "I'm sorry, Pippa. That was stupid, really
stupid. I was just taking my frustration out on you. That's all it
was."

Philippa turned carefully to face her, fearful that her movement
would cause Kay to take her arm away. She passionately did not
want Kay to draw away from her. She wanted to cling to Kay's
warm, vibrant body, to put her arms around Kay's neck and kiss
her lips, those soft, smiling lips only a few inches from her own.
Even as she was aware of these feelings she was shocked,
astonished. Since her mother's death she had exchanged kisses
with no one except for the polite pecks that were expected by
Elaine and other women of her acquaintance, and then only when
she could not avoid them. Never in her life had she felt such a
profound desire to kiss someone as she now felt she wanted to kiss
Kay, lingeringly, conveying by the pressure of her own lips the
heat of love that swelled in her heart. She stood still, scarcely

breathing, paralyzed by the intensity of her wish to prolong the moment.

It was Kay who made the first move. As if irresistably attracted, she leaned closer and gently pressed her lips on Philippa's, lingering for a moment before she drew back.

"Don't be angry with me, Pippa. You know that I say silly things when I'm upset."

Philippa, still unable to speak, watched as she went back to the sofa bed and dropped down onto it. Kay said, "She is such a possessive, jealous bitch that she can love no one but herself."

Her mind has gone back to Elaine and Stafford, thought Philippa, with a pang of jealousy. "She will do everything she can to keep you away from him."

"I was counting on the fact that eventually he would leave the hospital and then she would not be able to control what he does and who sees him."

Philippa's voice was sharp. "You deceive yourself. She does not need to imprison him to control what he does." Philippa plunged on, knowing that she was rending and tearing at Kay's feelings, helpless to prevent herself. "Perhaps it is true that Elaine loves no one but herself. I do not think that is so. She does love Stafford. But Stafford loves no one but himself. He married Elaine because he knew he was getting a rich wife who doted on him. Do you think he is going to make any sacrifice now—for you?"

Kay's eyes glowed at her strangely as she said, "You'd do better to leave well enough alone."

But Philippa could not stop herself. "Do you suppose this is the first time he has got himself involved with a woman so that he needed her help to disentangle himself? If you suppose that, let me disabuse you. It is not."

She stopped with a sharp intake of breath as she saw that Kay was twisting her tightly clasped hands and trembling. Kay managed to say in a stifled voice, "If you're not acting for Elaine, what are you doing?"

Philippa's rage began to recede. What was she doing? The strange, never before experienced emotion that had gripped her for the last moments began to lose its driving, overpowering force. As it receded she began to feel helpless, defenseless. The measured, calm nullity of her life up till that first moment of passionate longing she had faced two nights before seemed now to be returning, inexorably. She had not known before this that her life had been null. She had imagined it to be simply a rational, mind-dominated existence, free from the self-delusions that troubled more emotional people, delusions that were the creators of stress and unreasonable extremes of joy and gloom. The core of her life had become Kay and she had lost Kay forever. She gazed in anguish at Kay's abstracted, sad face.

Kay said in a quiet voice, "You've never been in love, have you? Because if you had, you would know that you don't choose to love somebody. Love is something that comes unbidden, not at the command of your own will. It's something—"

Philippa's voice interrrupted her, keen edged with the conscious desire to wound, "And you can't make someone else love you, no matter how strong your own love is."

Kay stared at her in surprise. She said slowly, "You don't believe he ever loved me."

"I know that he did not."

"How do you know when someone loves you?"

"I suppose, by the sacrifices he is willing to make."

"Sacrifices? You've got all the hang-ups, haven't you, Pippa? One is honorable, truthful, well-behaved under all provocation. One does not give in to one's emotions, but maintains one's dignity. One is certain that the true values of life are those of reason, moderate opinions, objectivity." Kay paused. She had mimicked Philippa's manner of speaking. Now she reverted to her own. "And it isn't like that at all. If you're in love, you don't give a damn for dignity, truthfulness, restrained behavior. What you want is the beloved. Yes, there are sacrifices. But they are sacrifices of things that no longer have the same value."

Philippa said angrily, "Stafford cares a great deal for outward appearances. He is upset about your public statements concerning him and your affair in Paris."

She thought Kay was going to rouse and lash out at her. But after a moment's flash of anger her head dropped again, the pale blonde hair hanging about her face. Oh, Kay, Kay! she cried silently.

Kay said, "If you're not Elaine's messenger, why are you saying all this?"

Philippa burst out, "Because I cannot bear to see you grieving over a man who doesn't want you, who enjoyed you and now sees you only as an embarrassment. I cannot bear it! I cannot bear it!"

Kay looked at her first in astonishment and then with a faint smile. "Pippa, what are you saying? Pippa—" She broke off and gazed at Philippa for a while silently. Her eyes traveled to Philippa's suitcase. "You're going back to Deerfield now?"

"Yes. There is no longer any reason for me to stay with Elaine. Stafford will be home in a day or so."

"Does she know you have stopped to see me?"

"Yes. She wants you to give her the letters Stafford wrote to you. She is willing to give you money for them."

She waited, uneasily, for Kay's response. But Kay merely asked, "Is that really the reason you stopped by?"

"No."

Kay smiled. There was a trace of disdain in her eyes. "No, of course it isn't. You have just said you stopped by because you had promised to do so before you went back to Deerfield."

Goaded by her tone Philippa said, "That is not really the reason, either. I stopped by because I wanted to see you again. I did not want to go away and not see you again."

Kay accepted her reply without comment. Presently she said, "Why should I return them to her?"

"The letters—Stafford's letters?"

"He wrote them to me."

"I pointed that out to her. It makes no difference to her, she wants them back."

"He won't care."

Surprised and apprehensive at her indifference Philippa said, "What do you mean, Kay?"

"I mean he won't care. He knows I wouldn't use any letters against him. Besides—"

Philippa waited without speaking. Kay went on, "It's all water under the bridge to him. He just doesn't want to be embarrassed, that's all."

Philippa stared at her in surprise. "Have you talked to him?"

Kay said impatiently, "I told you that I have talked to him on the phone." She was silent for a while and then she went on in a neutral voice, "Pippa, I thought that this time, with Stafford, I had the real thing. I really did. I would not believe anyone, even you, when you said that Stafford wasn't really in love with me. He acted, when he first met me, as if he had just been waiting for me to come along. He told me he had married Elaine because she had been so much in love with him and that he had tried to make a go of his marriage with her, but she was too possessive, too overbearing. He was so considerate, so gentle. I thought that with him I would really enjoy sex, that it would really mean something, that when it came to the climax, it wouldn't all just evaporate and leave me high and dry, the way it always does. I was really surprised when it didn't work out. But I thought it was simply because we were not permanently together—because there was an obstacle—Elaine—that kept us separate. And besides, I thought, even if I don't ever get over this, with Stafford it wouldn't matter. I loved him and he loved me."

Philippa, raging inwardly, did not speak.

Kay said, "I still thought that when I put a call in for him at the hospital. I had trouble getting to him but in the end he got on the line."

She stopped and was silent so long that Philippa looked at her. She was staring into space, motionless. Philippa said harshly, "You were bound to find out sooner or later that Stafford would never leave Elaine and that she would never let go of him."

Kay's eyes came slowly round to her. She nodded indifferently. "I guess so. But I did not think that when I called him." She paused and then went on. "He wasn't upset. He wasn't angry. He told me that he couldn't see me for a while. We had to go underground, he said. We had to wait until all this blew over, let everybody forget about what had happened to him, what I had said on TV. We had to give Elaine time to recover from the shock of all this. He is very concerned about Elaine's state of mind. He has been very inconsiderate of her, he said. What he has just been through has shown him how selfish he has been, how loyal Elaine is, how much he owes her. He must make all this up to her."

As she went on speaking her voice became more bitter, more pain-ridden. Philippa, listening with nerves quivering from indignation, sympathy, love, said nothing.

Kay attacked her. "All right. Go ahead and say it. You were right. He has given me the brush-off. Elaine is too important. He has forgotten what happened between us in Paris. It was just something passing, he said, something we'll both treasure, won't we, he said. Now be a good girl and get out of my hair."

Philippa cried out. "Stop it, Kay! Stop it!"

At the sound of her voice Kay looked up soberly. "I'm sorry, Pippa. I couldn't help it. I had to get that out."

Philippa pulled herself together. "He feels safe with Elaine. This time he got into deeper water than he expected. He is very grateful that she rescued him."

"So he won't care whether I give him back the letters or not."

"Elaine said that he was not concerned about them, that he told her that he could get them back from you himself. But she does not want him to see you again. He has promised her he will not see you again. Therefore, it is I who must come and talk to you about them. Elaine is eager to have them. I think she wants to make sure that all evidence of this particular adventure of Stafford's is wiped out. Or perhaps she will keep them to hold over his head, to remind him in the future."

Kay's laugh was unsteady. "I'd give a good deal to have my own letters back. I hate to think of them in her hands. It's—it's awful to think of her reading what I said to Stafford. In fact, it's awful to think of him re-reading them now. God, Pippa, why do I always have to be such a fool?"

A fool? thought Philippa. A fool because she is ready to give such love? Aloud she said, "Not a fool, Kay. You've simply mistaken the person to whom you offered your love."

Kay said bitterly, "Isn't that being the supreme fool—trying to make a gift of myself to somebody who doesn't want me?"

Kay, Kay, thought Philippa, in anguish, can't you see I want you? I have never wanted anyone before in my life, but I want you.

Kay, watching her, thought, she just can't say what is really in her mind. She loves me. Every glance of her eyes—those grey, thoughtful, shy eyes—tells me that. I never thought I would ever see love like that in anybody's eyes. But she can't speak to me of it. Oh, Pippa!

Philippa said aloud, "Kay, don't you remember how you used to talk to me on the ship—that you always found yourself in a meaningless sexual relationship with any man you went out with, when you had no intention of doing so? You did not mention Stafford. You only spoke of someone who you really thought loved you, in spite of the fact that he was married to someone else?"

Kay said in a low voice, "I guess I am superstitious. I was afraid if I spoke his name out loud—if I said out loud that Stafford loved me, something would happen to break it all up. It didn't help, did it?"

"You must have doubted, underneath, that he did love you."

Kay raised her head and Philippa saw that her face was wet with tears. Philippa cried, "Oh, Kay, you were deceiving yourself even then and you knew it."

"Pippa, don't you understand? I had to make myself believe that he loved me. I had to believe that somebody loved me because I was me. I had to believe that so that I could convince myself that I had any value—any—"

She broke down and dropped her face into her hands. It's no good, she thought. I can't get Pippa involved in my affairs. She'd give me everything she could, I know that. Her money, her reputation, her love, herself. But where would that leave her? I'm not worth all that devotion. I wish I had a drink. She is wondering why I'm sober. She is watching me the way she did on the ship. She is worried sick. I can see it on her face.

Kay said aloud, "I've never told you the story of my life, have I?"

Philippa said, surprised, "No."

"Well, my parents were divorced when I was eight years old. They both married again, so I wound up with two fathers and two mothers and three grandfathers and four grandmothers. I was the only child in the whole lot."

"You shouldn't have felt neglected, then."

"Oh, I can't complain of that. My own mother did try to pay extra attention to me. My stepfather was a musician and he was very conscientious in teaching me to play the violin. I was good enough for the student orchestra when I got to college. My own father made plenty of money. I always had all the clothes and things I wanted. My stepmother had been a dress designer once and she knocked herself out to keep me on the best-dressed list. And my grandparents always invited me round, share and share alike, for holidays and vacations, so I wouldn't be underfoot with my parents."

"Are they all dead now?" Philippa asked, incredulous.

Kay laughed. "Oh, you mean—the past tense. No. I've got three grandparents left and my two sets of parents are very much alive. They all worry about me. I expect my mother is having a fit about all this publicity. My father would send me money if I asked him to. But I'm not going to. I've been on my own since I got out of college."

Philippa was silent and after a while Kay said, "Don't you see, Pippa? They were all taken up with each other. They wanted to be kind to me and they did love me, I'm sure, as a child is loved by

well-meaning adults. But somehow I got the idea fixed in my mind
that I would always be a fifth wheel. And I've always wanted to be
first. I just have to be first. You can say that's a commonplace.
Well, I suppose there are lots of people who have felt that way.
But most people don't seem to have any trouble adjusting—you
know, accepting the idea that they can be first for a while and
then being displaced or going on to somebody else themselves.
Like me with Stafford. He made me think I was first when we
were together in Paris."

"You mean, he allowed you to deceive yourself."

Kay gave her a long look and then suddenly said, "I do wish I
had a drink. Wouldn't you like one?"

"All right."

Kay smiled at her. "But I don't have any scotch. And I don't
have any cash left."

"That's not a problem. Where is the nearest liquor store?"

Kay told her and she left the apartment and went down the
street and bought a bottle. Kay had tossed the latchkay to her and
she let herself in when she got back. She found Kay sitting as
before, as if scarcely aware that she had been gone.

Philippa poured a couple of drinks and set one down in front of
Kay. Kay picked it up automatically and drank half of it off.

"You had better go slow, Kay. I'm sure you have had nothing
to eat today. Do you have any food here?"

Kay said carelessly, "There are some cans of soup on the shelf."

Philippa went into the kitchenette and reached down a can of
soup, opened it and emptied the contents into a saucepan. She set
places for two and in a few minutes brought two soup-plates and
put them on the table.

"Come and eat, Kay. Fasting won't help."

Kay rose slowly and came and sat at the table. They ate in
silence. When she had finished, Kay lit another cigarette and sat on
at the table, absorbed in thought. Philippa, restless, got up and
carried the plates back to the kitchen sink. Then she went
systematically around the room and emptied the over-flowing
ashtrays that encumbered every surface. Whoever regularly lived in
this apartment, she thought, must be as great a smoker as Kay.

Kay, watching her with brooding eyes, noticed the economy of
her gestures, the neatness of her habitual movements. Who would
ever have supposed, she thought, that I would find a passion for
orderliness soothing? I always thought I hated precise, exacting,

formality-ridden people. I always thought they were death to spontaneous feeling, that they never felt the uprising of life's juices. But I'm wrong. Or at least I was wrong about Pippa. She'd be surprised if I told her that I find comfort in those neat, spare gestures of hers. In her. In her dependability. She said she was coming back and she came. She'd never give an empty promise, never a careless Yes.

Kay said aloud, "Pippa, don't go back to Deerfield tonight. Stay here with me. I'm afraid—I'm afraid to be alone."

And I am afraid to leave you alone, thought Philippa. How many sleeping pills have you got tucked away somewhere?

Aloud she said, "My flight has already left. There isn't another till morning. Don't you see? It is dark."

She gestured towards the open wondow. The daylight was fading quickly and the street lamps were already lit. She switched on the lamp near the coffee table.

Kay said, "Then stay here."

Philippa glanced around the room without replying.

"I'll sleep on the floor if you want the sofa to yourself," said Kay.

"Of course not."

They relapsed into silence. After a while Philippa asked, "Kay, don't you have any money?"

Kay, roused from brooding, said carelessly, "No. I can stay here for another week, I think. I'll just have to scrounge around for some cash—get an advance from somebody."

"Perhaps, then, you should consider Elaine's offer. She will pay well for Stafford's letters."

Kay was silent so long that Philippa looked at her anxiously. When Kay began to laugh, a low, helpless sort of laughter, Philippa said in alarm, "Kay, take hold of yourself. You've been brooding too long over all this. Here. See if this will help."

She poured out another drink and handed it to Kay. Kay took it automatically and drank. "I'm all right, Pippa. But I can't give you Stafford's letters."

"Why? Have you destroyed them?"

Kay's eyes lingered a while on hers and then dropped. "I never had any letters from Stafford—oh, some little non-committal notes that anybody could write to anyone else. The most compromising things in them were the mentions of times and places for us to meet. He sent me one note after he left Paris and another when he got back to Washington. I was still in London. I kept them for a while, just to have some tangible evidence of him, a scrap of his handwriting to remember our days and nights in Paris by. But in the end I threw them away. They were so meaningless." Kay broke off at the sight of Philippa's face. "Oh, I know! It's ghastly, isn't it, how stupid I've been. But before this you couldn't have convinced me that he wasn't as ardent as I was!"

Kay jumped up and began to walk distractedly round the room. Philippa got and intercepted her, catching her by her arms and forcing her to stand still.

"Kay, don't tear yourself up like this! Stafford isn't worth it! He has never given a serious thought to anyone else's feelings, not even Elaine's. Oh, yes! He is charming, he is delightful. He basks in a woman's adoration. I have seen him. He blossoms when an attractive woman throws herself at him."

"Throw myself at him! Of course. That's a good old Victorian phrase, isn't it? But it does fit the case, doesn't it?" Suddenly Kay tore her arms out of Philippa's grip and flung them around her neck. "Oh, Pippa! Tell me I'm not such a maudlin fool. Help me, Pippa!"

Philippa tenderly put her arms around her. "There now, don't let all this make you so unhappy, Kit-Kat."

Kay lifted her head from Philippa's shoulder to look at her. "You called me that once before."

"Yes."

Kay's tense body relaxed against Philippa's. "Pippa, can't you understand? Ever since I was a little girl, I've wanted to be first and only with somebody, somebody who would give me a special kind of love, who wouldn't make me share them with somebody else."

"That's a common human need," said Philippa gently.

Her restraint irritated Kay. "I'm talking about me. You needn't be so impersonal. I'm me and I want somebody to love me as me. That is what I thought I had with Stafford. I thought he loved me as he hadn't loved anybody else."

Philippa said sharply, "What you are saying is that he had to love you, because you needed him to, because you had never found your ideal lover, and you had to have one. Wasn't that it? Well, you were looking in the wrong place."

Kay in response to the note in her voice, lifted her head again to look at her attentively. "Pippa, you want to tell me something, don't you? Why don't you say it? Pippa, you love me, don't you? Isn't that why you came here now?"

Philippa, suddenly shy, said "Yes."

Kay raised her hands and caught Philippa's head between them. "You're afraid to tell me. You think I won't love you. Isn't that it? Pippa, you've got lots of courage, but you're afraid of people, aren't you? Oh, yes, you are. You wouldn't be afraid if you had to confront somebody over a matter of right and wrong—if it weren't personal. Isn't that it? It's nothing for you to be the champion of somebody else's cause, but you can't speak for yourself."

Philippa tried to speak. "I–I–."

"You what?"

"I couldn't bear for you to reject me."

Kay's little laugh was gentle. "There! You've said it! Pippa, you've never touched anybody before to show them you loved them, have you? You've always stood at a distance—even if you did feel love. You've been afraid to touch anyone, haven't you?"

Philippa did not look at her. "It–I have wanted to be able to love somebody—passionately—but I've never dared look to see if anyone would love me. It—it seemed too–dangerous."

"A fire gets hotter when you bank it. And it turns to ashes, then." Kay let go of her and turned away. "I used to wonder, on the ship, why you were so forbearing with me, so understanding, considering how fastidious you are, how self-controlled, how cool and reasonable—all the things I'm not. It seemed to me then odd that you not only put up with me. You took care of me, you defended me when people said things you thought were unfair. Oh, it didn't escape my notice that you put me to bed when I was too drunk to stand up—you, who have never been drunk. You tried to comfort me when I was afraid of the storm. I can see the reason now. I used to think about all that after we parted. It gave me a warm, comfortable feeling to remember you, Pippa. And more than that. I began to wish you were somewhere close so that I could go to you for solace."

Philippa looked at her sidelong. Yes, she protested silently, but it is not simply as a foster mother with a nestling that I love you. I love you as a lover. I love you passionately, with my body as well as my mind and soul. You don't reject me, you don't deny me. Oh, Kay, is it only passive acceptance on your part?

She heard Kay's voice again. "If I could only get my own letters back. Pippa, do you suppose you could prevail on her to let me have them back? I can't buy them."

"You needn't." Philippa reached down to the floor to pick up her handbag which she had placed there by her chair. "I told Elaine that I did not think you would sell Stafford's letters. But perhaps you would be willing to exchange them for your own. I didn't think, Kay, that you wanted yours to stay in her hands." She held the letters out to Kay. "There are only four. Elaine says she supposes Stafford must have destroyed the others."

Kay took the letters from her and sat looking at them. With a wry smile she said, "Now you know what nonsense I can write when I think I'm in love."

"I?" Philippa cried with a note of horror in her voice.

Kay glanced up at her. "Didn't you read them? Or did Elaine read them to you?"

"No, of course I did not read them! And I would not have let Elaine read them to me, if she had tried to."

"Why not?"

"They are not addressed to me."

"Of course. That would stop you, wouldn't it? But it didn't stop Elaine."

"Stafford is not my husband. Perhaps if I had been in Elaine's shoes I would have done likewise. She has been tormented by them, Kay."

Kay studied her face. "Is there another reason you did not read them? Suppose they had been open before you and you could hardly have avoided them?"

Philippa flushed. "That did not arise."

"I said, if it had. You would not have read them then, either."

"No. I would not. I could not have borne to read what you had written to someone else you thought you loved."

After a moment's silence Kay said, "Pippa, you know what love is now, don't you?"

"Yes."

"It's not tidy and reasonable and—and controllable. Poor Pippa."

"How did you know that is what I felt?"

"Because of the way you handled the letters—as if they were poisonous to the touch."

After another silence Kay said, "Pippa, give me another drink."

"You've had enough already."

"I know it. But I need another. I've got to have some sleep, Pippa."

Reluctantly Philippa poured whiskey into her glass. Kay took a swallow and lay back on the open sofa bed. After a silence, during which Philippa thought she had fallen asleep, she said, speaking as if from faraway, "Pippa, you're not going away? You are not going to leave me?"

"No. I will stay right here."

"What about the letters?"

"They are yours. You can do with them what you want to."

"And if Elaine says she wants them back?"

"I'm not in the least concerned with Elaine. I shall tell her that I have given them to you. They are your letters, if they are not Stafford's. I can tell her that you've destroyed them."

Kay gave a drowsy laugh. "Good heavens, Pippa! Don't tell me you are learning how to lie!"

"As you say, Kay, there are some things you can sacrifice when you're in love because they lose their value."

Kay laughed again. "Who's making fun of whom now?" She suddenly got up from the sofa and stood weaving beside it. "I've got to go to the bathroom."

Philippa caught hold of her arm and guided her across the room. Kay said, "You've done this before, haven't you, Pippa?"

"Something like it," said Philippa, steadying her.

When they returned to the sofa bed Kay flung off her robe and threw herself down. She was asleep instantly. Philippa gazed down at her for a while. She is lovely, she thought, even if she is even thinner than she was on the ship. She is like a child, she is so careless of herself.

Gently Philippa drew up the covers and tucked them around her. Then she walked to the open window and stood in the cool breeze that had sprung up with the setting of the sun. There was a touch of winter in the air and it made her shiver. As she stood there, absorbed in contemplation of the last few days, she realized that she no longer inhabited the same world she had known before she had boarded the ship in Southampton. The texture, the feel, the sounds of this present world of hers were new and yet already so intimately familiar that her old world appeared in retrospect to be strange, muted, dim. She thought suddenly of the lighted tank of an aquarium, where the underwater plants wavered and trembled in the motion of a hidden current and an occasionally sightless fish flirted past to be lost again in the darker corners. In that world she had been a spectator. Its sounds and motions had been outside of herself, observed, recorded in impersonal terms.

She turned back into the room and stood beside the sofa bed watching Kay asleep. Why not, she thought. Why shouldn't she come with me to Deerfield? For a while she is going to need a temporary means of earning money to live on, till she can pick up the threads of her professional life. She smiled to herself. Kay would say that I have at last learned to act on my own, not according to the rules someone else taught me. She can come to Deerfield and be a consulting monitor in the new media seminar. That's Livingstone's department. He's been waiting to invite somebody who is in the news—is active in something relevant, he calls it. She was the film editor of *The Suburbanite.* Trudy remembered that. And then there is the subsidy for speakers for the Student Union. The students would be delighted to have a figure in a recent scandal involving the government. And she can stay with me.

A month ago she would not have dared think of such a thing. She would have dismissed it as impossible, too provocative, too potentially explosive, too fraught with danger. She almost laughed aloud when she thought of it. Philippa Weir, the bulwark of conservatism, the consummate scholar, the—yes, bloodless epitome of reason, reserve, unemotionalism. She thought of her apartment. In her mind's eye she saw the orderly sittingroom with its Sheraton-style furniture and blue Chinese silk rug, the bedroom with its white and gold painted bed and dressing table and chairs. Everyone thought it, she knew, the chaste nest of the campus' most chaste inhabitant. She imagined it littered with Kay's garments, Kay's cigarette ashes, Kay's carelessly dropped books and papers. How surprised Trudy would be—

She paused to think of Trudy. Yes, even Trudy did not frighten her. I've learned a particular kind of courage, she thought, a particular kind of self-respect, that I did not know existed. I'm alive. I'm a whole human being. And it is Kay who has done this.

She looked at the electric clock. It was almost midnight. Philippa was conscious of fatigue. She had thought vaguely of taking off her shoes and spending the night in the armchair. But now, looking down at the deeply sleeping Kay, she made up her mind to go to bed.

Slowly she took off her clothes and hung them on some empty hangers in the hall closet. When she had finished in the bathroom she returned to the sofabed in her nightgown, turned off the lamp and lay down on the outer half of the bed. Kay had rolled over towards the wall with her face in the pillow.

Philippa lay on her back, watching the pattern of light cast through the window onto the ceiling by the street lamp. Kay did not stir. She could hear her regular breathing near her ear and suddenly felt an exquisite sense of intimacy, of being close to the one person in the world with whom she could share herself. She luxuriated in the warmth of Kay's body, the faint reek of Kay's breath and sweat, the confiding pressure of Kay's weight when she unconsciously rolled over towards her.

Philippa did not know when she woke or what had wakened her. The night was very quiet with few sounds from the street, so she supposed it must be well towards daybreak. She had known, even before she had fully roused, that she was in bed with Kay, that it was Kay's body that pressed against her own. She lay consciously still, anxious not to waken Kay. Her mind reverted to the events of the last few days, to Elaine. She found that she shied away from the thought of Stafford, of Kay's infatuation. It will take me some time, she thought, to conquer the feeling of jealous rage that threatened to spring up if she dwelt upon that.

Kay suddenly stirred beside her. Kay's voice, sleep-laden, said, "Pippa?" She felt Kay's hands on her body, searching over her for reassurance. "Oh, Pippa! You didn't go away!"

Philippa, turmoil rising in her, said as quietly as she could, "I said I would stay."

Kay subsided against her. "Yes. And what you say you will do, you're always going to do, aren't you?"

They were both quiet for a while, Philippa striving to quell the turmoil in herself, Kay limp and still. But then Kay raised herself on her elbow. In the faint light Philippa was aware of her face just above her own.

"Pippa, hold me. Don't just lie there."

And Philippa, with a violence she could never have imagined, seized Kay's body in her arms.

Publications of
THE NAIAD PRESS, INC.
P.O. Box 10543 • Tallahassee, Florida 32302
Mail orders welcome. Please include 15% postage.

Mrs. Porter's Letter by Vicki P. McConnell. A mystery novel.
224 pp. ISBN 0-930044-29-0 .... $6.95

To the Cleveland Station by Carol Anne Douglas. A novel.
192 pp. ISBN 0-930044-27-4 .... $6.95

The Nesting Place by Sarah Aldridge. A novel. 224 pp.
ISBN 0-930044-26-6 .... $6.95

This Is Not for You by Jane Rule. A novel. 284 pp.
ISBN 0-930044-25-8 .... $7.95

Faultline by Sheila Ortiz Taylor. A novel. 140 pp.
ISBN 0-930044-24-X $6.95

The Lesbian in Literature by Barbara Grier. 3rd ed.
Foreword by Maida Tilchen. A comprehensive bibliog.
240 pp. ISBN 0-930044-23-1 .... ind. $7.95
inst. $10.00

Anna's Country by Elizabeth Lang. A novel. 208 pp.
ISBN 0-930044-19-3 .... $6.95

Lesbian Writer: Collected Work of Claudia Scott
edited by Frances Hanckel and Susan Windle. Poetry. 128 pp.
ISBN 0-930044-22-3 .... $4.50

Prism by Valerie Taylor. A novel. 158 pp.
ISBN 0-930044-18-5 .... $6.95

Black Lesbians: An Annotated Bibliography compiled by
JR Roberts. Foreword by Barbara Smith. 112 pp.
ISBN 0-930044-21-5 .... ind. $5.95
inst. $8.00

The Marquise and the Novice by Victoria Ramstetter.
A novel. 108 pp. ISBN 0-930044-16-9 .... $4.95

Labiaflowers by Tee A. Corinne. 40 pp. $3.95

Outlander by Jane Rule. Short stories, essays.
207 pp. ISBN 0-930044-17-7 .... $6.95

Sapphistry: The Book of Lesbian Sexuality by
Pat Califia. 195 pp. ISBN 0-930044-14-2 .... $6.95

Lesbian-Feminism in Turn-of-the-Century Germany.
An anthology. Translated and edited by Lillian Faderman
and Brigitte Eriksson. 120 pp. ISBN 0-930044-13-4 .... $5.95

(continued on next page)

The Black and White of It by Ann Allen Shockley.
Short stories. 112 pp. ISBN 0-930044-15-0 $5.95

At the Sweet Hour of Hand-in-Hand by Renée Vivien.
Translated by Sandia Belgrade. Poetry. xix, 81 pp.
ISBN 0-930044-11-8 $5.50

All True Lovers by Sarah Aldridge. A novel. 292 pp.
ISBN 0-930044-10-X $6.95

The Muse of the Violets by Renée Vivien. Poetry. 84 pp.
ISBN 0-930044-07-X $4.00

A Woman Appeared to Me by Renée Vivien. Translated
by Jeannette H. Foster. A novel. xxxi, 65 pp.
ISBN 0-930044-06-1 $5.00

Lesbiana by Barbara Grier. Book reviews from
The Ladder. iv, 309 pp. ISBN 0-930044-05-3 $5.00

Cytherea's Breath by Sarah Aldridge. A novel. 240 pp.
ISBN 0-930044-02-9 $6.95

Tottie by Sarah Aldridge. A novel. 181 pp.
ISBN 0-930044-01-0 $5.95

The Latecomer by Sarah Aldridge. A novel. 107 pp.
ISBN 0-930044-00-2 $5.00

A VOLUTE BOOK
NAIAD PRESS, INC.
P.O. Box 10543
Tallahassee, Florida 32302

All Naiad Press Books listed in this book can be purchased by
mail, as well as Valerie Taylor's three titles.

**Journey to Fulfillment, A World without Men and Return to
Lesbos**
$3.95 each plus 15% postage and handling—minimum 75¢.

NAME _____

ADDRESS _____

CITY _____ STATE _____ ZIP _____

BOOK(S) _____

_____

TOTAL ENCLOSED $ _____